OUR KIND OF LOVE

SHANE MORGAN

ONE

Micah

Broken. Outcast. Trash.

Several months ago, that was me. Mitchel Stephens. Those words described *my* life.

Staring out the bus window, I reflect on everything that led me to this point, like how I had to keep my head down whenever I left my house. And the way people regarded me—screwed up their faces, whispered, and pointed fingers—was disheartening. I couldn't even go to the grocery store without falling under someone's microscope.

That was my life in the small town of Haxtun, Colorado. I returned from juvie lost, with no clue what to do next, even though my counselor at the detention center had sat me down during a session and told me the best solution to my problems.

"Mr. Stephens, you have to try to move on. Leave the past behind."

Easy for him to say. I'd dealt with too much. First, Dad turned his back on me. Then Grams died during my time away. The pain from losing her hurt like hell.

She'd been both parents to me. She did what they couldn't do: stick around and love me unconditionally.

Move on?

Where would I go? What would I do?

I'd let Grams down. After everything she did for me, I ignored her warnings about Jason and did what I wanted. My selfish decisions led me to where she didn't want me to end up: in trouble.

The kind of trouble people don't forget. Ever. The kind that turned so-called friends and neighbors into judges who scrutinized every single move.

It also gave them some power, enabling them to treat me like nothing.

Worse than nothing. As if I didn't fucking exist.

Move on, huh?

I finally had no choice. I took my counselor's advice and moved out of Haxtun, leaving behind the memories of my grams and my past life.

Wanting a fresh start somewhere else, I hopped on a train to Illinois, trying to get as far away as possible, and wound up in Georgetown. After two days of searching, I found a job as a waiter at a restaurant.

Those first few months were all right. I met some interesting people, had fun with girls, and ultimately, I got by. Then, it began two nights ago.

The dreams. The bad memories. They crept up on me, and the itch to leave spread throughout my body.

So here I am now, my old duffel bag draped over my shoulder, climbing off a Greyhound bus a few days after deciding on my next destination: Newport, a seaside city in Rhode Island. It seems like a nice enough place, just as far from Colorado as Illinois was. No one will know me here, either. I might be running away, but that doesn't matter. I want to keep going. Maybe traveling will help me shake my guilt.

The fierce afternoon sun bites my bare arms. I haven't changed my gray T-shirt and black jeans in two days. My armpits feel sweaty. I seriously need a shower. Fast.

I walk into the sparse transportation center, cringing at the mellow pop song blaring *No Place Like Home* from the speakers. How ironic.

Purchasing a bus pass, I stand around and wait for the next trolley. Within minutes, it pulls up outside. I hop on and sit in the back. According to the map app on my phone, this one will stop at the corner down from my new digs.

The ride isn't too long. I jump off the trolley at Pelham Street and look around. Nice area. The road's a bit patchy in some parts, though.

I approach the blue multi-family house at the corner of the street. After paying the landlord enough Franklins to cover the first and last month's rent, I climb to the third floor, my sneakers squeaking on the hardwood stairs. There's a small window up top, but I can't see anything with the giant tree blocking the view.

Wiping my feet on the rug outside the door, I unlock it and step inside. The air smells like wood and fresh paint. I pause after closing the door and take in the sizable furnished studio.

Two double-hung windows show the houses across the street and a park in the distance. The kitchen's small. A queen bed on the other side. Overall, the place is the right size for one person—for me. It's my home, for now.

Settling down on the dark leather couch, I call up a restaurant hiring for the summer. The owner sounds nice, and I feel confident about the job since she wants me to stop by Monday morning.

I shower, haul on a t-shirt and gym shorts, and order takeout. Once I finish eating, I stroll around the neighborhood, ending up at the park near the harbor.

I'm just in time to watch the sunset, something I haven't bothered to do in months. For some reason, I feel compelled to observe this one.

Relaxing on a park bench, I stare at the orange and yellow burning together on the horizon. I appreciate the natural beauty for a while until something, or rather *someone*, more captivating graces my view.

A young woman, seeming lost in thought, walking barefoot across the seawall made of rustic red pebble stones separating sand from the sea. Her body shivers with each step against the ocean breeze. Her cute blue dress with floral prints flares modestly just below her knees. She pays no attention to anything else around her, unaware that my eyes are trained on her every move.

As the setting sun slants across her tanned legs, she pauses and stares into the distance. She flips her long, light brown hair off her shoulders, the strands falling elegantly down her back.

Caught up, I lean forward, my gaze fixed on nothing but her. *Turn.* I wish she'd turn and let me see her face entirely. Even my heart begins to thud with anticipation.

8

Finally, as if hearing me, she twists, her attention riveted on something on the street to her left. *Oh, come on, turn toward me.*

My breath glitches as she pivots fully this time, and I catch a glimpse. She's beautiful, but not in a shallow way. Something about her intrigues me.

What am I doing? Why am I just sitting here watching her?

Snapping back to my senses, I spring from the bench and start over, hoping she won't run when I tell her how angelic she is before my eyes. *Geez.* That's corny as hell, but I don't care. I have to talk to this girl.

I'm almost there when the loud *beep-beep* of a car draws her attention. As she turns, the motion stops me in my tracks. A wide smile spreads across her pink lips, and like an idiot, I convince myself she's smiling at me.

Realization bites me on the ass when she rushes past me like I'm invisible, heading for the red jeep parked on the street waiting for her.

She didn't see me. Like seriously?

I stand there watching as she quickens inside the jeep, shuts the door, and the driver takes off. Now I feel like crap because I wasted time and missed the chance to talk to her. I wonder if I'll ever even see her again.

Disappointment has me hunching my shoulders. I walk from the sand onto the grass and sit back on the bench, dumping grains from my flip-flops.

I run my fingers through my messy hair and start laughing at myself. *Why did I get so riled up?* That girl's simply another pretty face. I've seen many in the last few months. We meet, hook up, and I move on.

The last thing I want is a girlfriend. I'm a no-commitment type of guy. None of them ever took the guilt away.

But how I'm feeling at the moment is wild. Just one look at that girl, and I want to stick around and get to know her. That's if I ever see her again.

TWO

Reign

SO FAR, my summer has been a disaster. I'd hoped my parents would sponsor a trip to reward my hard work after graduating high school a week ago. Instead, I'm spending my days laboring at *Captain's Choice* while my friends are partying in the Bahamas.

Well, I guess I shouldn't complain since there's no way my parents can afford it. Most of their money went toward my college tuition because I slacked off and didn't get a scholarship as planned, and they had to cover other expenses, too.

Captain's Choice isn't as hot on the block as it used to be. Some days, it's up. Sometimes, it's slow. Business is unpredictable, but it still has its regulars. So, if I help until the end of July, I can at least go to Miami with Claudia before starting at the University of Rhode Island in the fall. We've been planning for God knows how long. There's no way I'll miss out on *that* trip.

Sighing, I wipe sweat from my forehead with the back of my hand, thinking how my former classmates are having the time of their lives right now in the

Bahamas. Lucky brats. They have their wealthy mommies and daddies to spoil them rotten.

I scoff at the thought because who am I kidding? I wouldn't enter the ocean, and I'm not a drinker. I'm not missing out on much.

Florida's supposed to be the trip to cure me. Claudia swears she'll find a way for me to overcome my issues with the ocean. I doubt it, but it'll be fun, just the two of us spending time together before she leaves for college in New York.

An awful ache erupts in my shoulders. I stop cleaning the tables, toss the towel over the back of one of the chairs, and plop down in it to take a break.

Gawd! My shirt's sticking to my clammy skin. It has to be the hottest morning since June began. Right now, I wouldn't mind a winter storm.

I should finish out here and get back inside to cool down in the Air Conditioner.

As I'm about to ease up from the chair, I hear handclaps and Mom's demanding voice ordering me back to work. "It's almost opening, Reign. Stop lazing around. Come on."

Grumbling, I push up from the chair, snatch the towel off the back, and make for inside the restaurant.

Mom eyes me from head to toe, taking in my flats, knee-length shorts, and t-shirt. Before I can step past her, she tugs on my arm and slows me down.

"Honey, I'd appreciate it if you wore appropriate clothing to work. You're not at the beach," she scolds.

I dip my head back and exhale in exasperation. "Come on, Mom. *Captain's Choice* isn't a formal restaurant. It's *way* too hot for long sleeves. The dress code should be more casual."

"Don't give me that excuse." She folds her arms. "I have uniforms for summer. You choose not to wear them."

"Because they're plain," I retort, smirking. "How about listening to my suggestion about letting *me* design the uniforms?"

With an eye roll, Mom untangles her arms and slaps my elbow lightly. "I would never let you do that. Next thing I know, the entire staff will be in ripped jeans and hippie-looking tops."

"Huh?" I glance down and screw up my face as I look back at her. "This isn't hippie-looking."

"No, but it's still unprofessional." She smiles.

"I think—"

"Excuse me." The husky voice startles us.

I peer over Mom's shoulder at the guy approaching and almost faint. Talk about attractive. He's tall, a good six feet two compared to my itty-bitty five-three. From how the fitted gray t-shirt hugs his broad shoulders, toned arms, and bulging chest, it seems he works out.

I like how his dark brown hair is cropped at the sides with longer layers on top, highlighting its natural wavy texture.

Bringing my eyes back to his handsome, chiseled face, I can't shake the feeling that I've seen him before. No clue as to where, though. Staring at him incites an uncontrollable rush throughout my body. I should not be feeling anything like that.

I clear my thoughts in time to hear why he's looking for my mom.

"I'm Micah Delaney. I called last Friday about the position, and you told me to stop by this morning," he explains.

"Oh, yes," Mom replies enthusiastically. "Thanks for coming. I'm Sophia Aldridge, the owner."

He shakes her outstretched hand. "It's nice to meet you, Ms. Aldridge. You said the position is only for the summer and is available immediately?"

I can't get over the deep, sexy, and smooth voice leaving his mouth.

"Well, that's if I decide to give you a shot," Mom says.

I'm not sure what transpires afterward since I block everything out while I continue to study him. *Memorize him is more like it.* There's something enthralling about Micah Delaney. Even though he appears polite and eager to work, his smile seems forced. His body language reflects a guy who is well-guarded. *Yeah, something's going on behind those gorgeous sea-blue eyes.*

"And this is Reign," Mom introduces.

I snap out of my admiring as Micah wrinkles his thick brows, narrows his eyes, and slowly extends his hand to me. It's almost as if he's seen me before, too.

Then something odd happens, something that isn't supposed to happen at the touch of our hands. Butterflies wake in my stomach and my pulse quickens.

A slow smile tilts his lips like he's genuinely amazed by me. His overall expression has relaxed. He looks more confident now regarding me.

Weird.

I'm suddenly hyper-aware that we're still shaking hands. Oddly, I don't want to let go. Micah's touch is warm—*duh, it's a blazing hot summer day*. No, this is more like a sensual warmth. The kind of heat that not only arouses a girl but also makes her feel safe. Protected.

"Micah." I drop his hand fast at Mom's voice. "Walk with me to the office. We'll talk more."

As he turns away, I can't believe the disappointment inside. *Frick!* He's just another good-looking guy. I see them every day around here. And Nate is just as hot.

Yeah, remember Nate, your boyfriend?

Watching as Micah wanders off with Mom, I almost jump out of my skin when he glances back at me, delight dancing in his eyes before he turns the corner inside the restaurant.

I zap out of whatever that was and return to work. I can't believe I'm gawking at a hot guy when I have a boyfriend. Damn.

Finished on the deck, I bring the cleaning supplies inside and put them away. I notice Aislin is preparing the bar because John isn't in yet. We open at ten, so he still has half an hour to avoid my mom's wrath.

My cell phone buzzes in my shorts pocket the second I sit on one of the bar stools. Taking it out to check the screen, I see a text from Nate.

Hey babe.
I'm stopping by this afternoon
since I'll be around the harbor.
Cool?

15

I want to tell him not to drop by while I'm at work because no one here likes it, especially Mom. She also thinks it's unprofessional for an employee to have her boyfriend flirting with her in front of customers.

Still, I can't say no. We haven't seen each other much since graduating, and Nate works part-time in the Mayor's office doing who knows what. His father helped him land the position.

He's a sweet boyfriend. He's always been good to me, even staying behind instead of going to the Bahamas with our classmates. I don't know how to turn him down. Except for sex. We haven't reached that part yet.

I send him a simple reply.

Okay.

"Boyfriend coming by today?" Aislin asks, sounding annoyed.

Sticking my phone in my pocket, I lift my head to see her glaring at me. "Um, yeah. Are you fine with that?"

"Whatever." She cuts her brown eyes and turns her back on me, checking the remaining level of alcohol in a bottle. "Don't leave your tables hanging so you two can fool around. It'll probably be a busy day, and we're already short-staffed," she grumbles.

"Well, not for long," I throw back, thinking of Micah. "Looks like we'll have a new addition until Marie returns."

"Oh, goodie," she chirps.

Irritated, I slide off the stool and walk back outside to the deck. Aislin hasn't been as cool as when she started working here last year. She won't tell me what's eating at her, yet she keeps giving me the stink eye, frowning whenever I mention Nate.

I lean over the wooden railing and stare at the calm water below, thinking how badly I want to travel. But with my fears holding me back, it's sad that I'll probably never have the chance to see the world.

I'm worried about Mom, too. She won't tell me straight up, but I know something's wrong. She doesn't seem to love the restaurant business anymore.

That's all I ever deliberate on during my downtime at work. Unexpectedly, my mind drifts to Micah's enigmatic blue eyes. To the feel of his hand holding mine and the way he peeked back at me—without hesitation—as if I was worth a second glance.

Nate's never stared at me like that.

THREE

Micah

I CAN'T BELIEVE it's her—the girl from the park. *Reign.* I like that name. From how she looked at me, it appears she did glimpse me that day but doesn't appear to remember. Regardless, I'm curious about how she checked me out on the deck like she was studying my physique with those gorgeous hazel eyes. They're going to be hard to avoid.

Damn! That handshake was long. She didn't want to let go. Or maybe it's me. I didn't want to release that soft, tiny hand that fit perfectly in mine. The problem is that Reign is the boss lady's daughter, so I must keep my distance and maintain a professional relationship.

Upon entering the matchbox office at the back of the restaurant and glimpsing family photos on her desk, I realize my boss is married and should address her as Mrs. Aldridge.

She sits behind the desk and motions for me to get comfortable. While lowering in the chair, visions of her daughter fill my head again. I imagine wrapping my fingers around her long, cinnamon-brown hair and kissing those pink, plush lips. She'd probably feel so good under my body.

Shit. If I don't free my head of these dirty thoughts of what I'd like to do with her, my attraction could cause serious trouble. I mean, I'm sitting across from her mother. How disgusting of me.

In no time, Mrs. Aldridge starts questioning me about my previous work experiences. Her stern gaze makes me nervous. Her scrutiny is the kind that intimidates the hell out of people with shit to hide.

People like me.

Regardless, I do my best to appear calm. I want this job, especially if I can spend time with Reign.

"Wow, you've traveled a long way, moving from Colorado to Illinois and now to Rhode Island," she says, skimming my resume. "Is that why you don't mind working for just the summer? What about your previous job at Chang's Little Shanghai Restaurant? Any particular reason why you left? It doesn't look like you worked there for long, either. Only a few months."

I loosen the tightness in my throat to answer. "Well, I stopped working there because I wanted a change. I like to travel, and Newport appealed to me when I saw pictures of the city online."

Her head goes up and down in a slow nod. "My daughter wants to travel, too." I try hard to hide the strange thrill of hearing that. "She's mentioned it a few times. I guess most young people do."

Hmm. I'd love a gorgeous travel companion like Reign. "That's great," I hurry to say, stifling my inappropriate thoughts. "Has she gone anywhere yet?"

Mrs. Aldridge's pale blue eyes widen, and her head dips back. Then she glances down at my resume and mutters, "No. She has a lot to deal with now, especially getting through college and learning to make firm decisions about her future. There's no time to play around."

"Oh, good for her. Is she going to major in travel?"

"No," she answers dryly. "Reign decided to study business. That's best for her, I guess."

There's something about her response that's unnerving. But it's none of my business. I shouldn't be asking the lady about her daughter. *What the hell, Micah? You're here for work.*

My throat tightens as she pops her head up and looks me dead in the eye. I have to ready myself for her other questions.

"It all seems fine to me," she says. "There's no reason I shouldn't consider you, and since I need someone at this very moment for our busy days ahead, I have no problem letting you start right away."

Relief floods me, and I manage a relaxed grin. The interview went easier than I thought.

I'm about to thank her for the opportunity when Mrs. Aldridge says, "Do you mind if I run a background check? It's mandatory for new employees."

Shit! How did I not think about that at all? Oh, right, my position at the Chinese restaurant in Georgetown was a no-questions-asked-just-do-the-work type of job.

I swallow hard before I ask in a low tone, "Even if it's only for the summer?"

That must sound suspicious because she tilts her head to one side and narrows her gaze. "Well, yes. Is something wrong?"

"No," I answer fast. "Nothing's wrong. That's completely fine."

"I'm sure it won't take long. As I've said, I'd love for you to start immediately. My other waitress won't return until after summer, and it's been hectic with only Aislin and Reign. Aislin has summer classes, so she's cut her hours back. The position will be perfect since you're looking for temporary work. Do you want the job?"

My mind is still stuck on that stupid background check the entire time she's talking. Once she runs it, Mrs. Aldridge will discover that I'm using Grams' maiden name and that Micah isn't my first name either.

"Yes..."

Why can't she be like my previous boss? He didn't care about those things, only if I could keep up with his fast-paced business, *and* he paid me in cash. Hopefully, she'll do the same.

"So," she breaks through my thoughts, sounding enthusiastic again. "Are you ready to get started?"

"Yes, ma'am." I stand and shake her hand. "Thank you."

She gestures for me to exit the office, leading me to the employees' room. After giving me two uniforms and a locker, I follow her to the kitchen, where she introduces me to her chef, Clark Fernandez. He looks in his mid-forties, like Mrs. Aldridge. He shares that he was born in Puerto Rico and moved to the States as a

21

kid with his father. Another place I'd love to travel to someday.

Afterward, I walk back to the employees' room to change into one of the uniforms—black pants and a white dress shirt with the restaurant's name in blue stitching over the shirt pocket. I enter the dining area, and Mrs. Aldridge refreshes my memory of placing the utensils and centerpieces on the tables.

She's about to head back to her office when the door opens, and a frazzled-looking guy enters.

Mrs. Aldridge utters a low hum, checks her watch, and frowns at him. Without a word, she shakes her head, marches past the bar, and veers to the passage that stretches back to her office.

The guy releases the breath he's been holding, strolls over to the bar, and puts down his small black bag. He doesn't even bother with me as he steps past and strides around back, possibly to change into a uniform.

While setting down napkins and water glasses, I glimpse Reign out of the corner of my eye. She isn't being too discreet, either, staring at me every so often. She still looks as if she's trying to remember my face.

"Hey," a raspy voice calls out from behind me.

I spin around to see a girl with boyish, short blonde hair and a silver nose ring.

"Hey," I reply.

Edging closer, she lifts her hand to shake mine as she introduces herself, "Aislin."

"Micah," I say with a half-smile. Her face remains serious as she reads me. Growing slightly uncomfortable, I ask, "Is there anything you need my help with?"

She shrugs. "I was just being courteous, unlike John." She nods in that direction. "He's the bartender. He can be a prick sometimes, but it's because he's going through some stuff."

"It's fine." Honestly, I don't care. We all have shit we're dealing with in our lives.

Aislin turns around. Before returning to whatever she was doing, she peers over her shoulder and winks at me, saying with a smirk, "You're cute."

"Thanks... I guess."

She saunters off, and I resume what I was doing before.

Around noon, the restaurant starts picking up. While taking an old couple's order, some guy wanders in. There's a definite arrogant vibe about him.

The restaurant doesn't have a hostess. Aislin is closest to him from the door, so I assume she'll tell him to sit wherever there's an empty table. She only glances behind at him, swivels instantly, and pretends he's not even there as she continues to focus on her table. He doesn't look all too interested in her, either. If I didn't know better, I'd say there's tension between them—the 'we slept together last night, and you didn't even bother to call me' kind of tension.

I'm about to walk over and guide him to a table but decide against it when he starts for the deck, seeming to have found the reason why he's here.

Reign.

No. Screw me. I don't have a chance now.

A cocky grin spreads across his pretty boy face. He must be her boyfriend. No surprise there. She's too gorgeous to be single.

23

Walking over to Reign, he drapes his arms around her waist from behind and kisses her on the cheek. With no regard for the fact that she's at work, he pulls her away after she pours a glass of water for a customer and tows her to the railing.

Reign smiles awkwardly at him as if she doesn't want him here. *Interesting.*

I observe them on the way to the bar to plug in my customers' orders. He never takes his hands off her. It makes me cringe somewhat. As if she senses me, Reign looks over and catches me staring.

Oops.

I drop my eyes and put in the orders. That guy probably noticed, too. He has nothing to worry about when it comes to me. I'm not a girlfriend stealer.

Still, that kiss bothers me for some reason, and I detest how he rests his hands on her hips like he's staking his claim.

What a territorial prick.

FOUR

Reign

"WHO'S THAT GUY?" Nate asks, eyeing Micah with suspicion.

"New employee. Why? Are you pissed I have so many hot guys around me?"

He scoffs. "Not in the least. I just haven't seen him before. Anyway, I know you only have room for me. So, are you coming by Lucas' tonight?"

I wrinkle my brows while searching my head. Seeing how lost I am, he reminds me, "It's his birthday. He's throwing a party, remember?"

"Oh, right. Um, I don't know, Nate. The restaurant closes at ten. By then, I'll be pretty tired."

He furrows his brows, seeming ticked off by my excuse. "I'm sure your mom can let you slip away earlier if you tell her it's for me. Sophia loves me as your boyfriend, right? Besides..." A sneaky grin appears on his clean-shaven face. "I've been looking forward to it 'cause I was hoping we'd sneak out of the party and spend the night at my house."

That's a no-no. I've known Nate since junior high school, but we've only started dating two months before graduation. I'm not ready to take our relationship to the next level.

"I'm sorry," I say. "Even if I get the chance to go out tonight, I don't know if I want to sleep over—"

"Oh, geez. I'm not insinuating anything, Reign." He sputters a short laugh and kisses me lightly on the forehead. "It's okay. Since you'll be working most of the summer and I'm busy with my stuff, I just wanted to hang out with you alone. We aren't even going to the same college."

I lower my gaze to the half-empty jar in my hand. Nate lifts my chin and sticks a loose strand of hair behind my ear. "Hey, it's fine. Don't look so worried."

Gazing into his brown eyes, I smile and tell him softly, "You should go. I'm working. I'll ask Mom, okay?"

Nate briefly runs his thumb across my bottom lip and nods. "Cool. See you later then." He says it confidently because he knows I'll be at Lucas' house. That's me, always trying to keep him happy. I feel like I have to work extra hard to make up for my lack of intimacy.

I watch as he strides for the exit, steps outside, hops in his Porsche, and drives off.

He's upset. I can tell. No matter how he tries to seem okay with waiting, he's not. But I won't sleep with him, not yet. Not until it feels right.

For some strange reason, I glance at Micah before bringing the jar back to the bar to refill it with water. He was watching Nate and me earlier, and his reaction seemed odd. If anything, he appeared... disappointed.

On my way to the kitchen to check my table's order, Mom catches me in the passage.

"What's up?" I ask innocently, fearing she saw Nate leave.

"I'm heading to the craft shop to see your father. Will you at least change into a uniform before it gets busy? I mean, look at Micah." She nods in his direction. I slant and take in his appearance. "Even he has changed into my uniform. Set an example and do the same."

"Okay, Mom," I cave.

Her lips curl into a satisfied grin. I can see wrinkles at the corners of her blue eyes as she beams at me with pride.

Remembering Lucas' party, I ask softly, "Mom, is it okay if I head out an hour early to go to Nate's cousin's birthday party tonight?"

Her smile falters as she considers it. She lets out a long gush of air and firmly answers, "No. You leave at the same time as the others. How would it look for Aislin, John, and Micah if I let you out early for a party? I don't think so, Reign. You leave at ten. End of discussion."

I bite down on my bottom lip, fuming. She pats my arm and continues toward the exit.

There's nothing I can say in protest. Even though I want to be a good girlfriend and make an effort in our relationship, I don't want to disappoint my parents.

Mary wouldn't. And since she's no longer here because of me, I have to take her place. I have to be the obedient daughter.

FIVE

Micah

BY CLOSING time that night, I was exhausted. I carry the last trash bag to the dumpster, change into my jeans and t-shirt, and then head out for the evening.

Walking into the main dining area, I spot Mrs. Aldridge and John at the bar reviewing papers. Aislin is also on her way out. She waves to me before she steps out the door.

"Thanks again, Mrs. Aldridge," I say, moseying to the exit.

They look up at me, and she smiles approvingly. "Good job today, Micah," she says. "It'll just be you and Reign for most of tomorrow morning. Aislin starts in the afternoon, so it's great that you can manage when it gets busy."

"Yeah, man. Good work," John adds. It's the first thing he's said to me all day.

"Thanks. See you both."

I pivot and step out the door, just in time to see Reign climb into the passenger side of the red jeep that picked her up at the park the other day. I start up the street, hurrying to catch the next trolley in the square.

Seconds later, I hear a honk and slow my stride as the jeep pulls up beside me. The fiery redhead driving flashes me her pearly whites, wetting her lips while eyeing me up and down flirtatiously.

"Hey there, cutie," she says.

"Hey." I stick my hands in my pockets.

Reign leans forward and asks me, "You want a ride home, Micah?"

I shake my head. "Nah, it's all right. I'll hop on the trolley."

"Nonsense," the redhead counters. "Take the free ride and save your money. I don't mind."

"Ah..." I glance up the road. Any minute now, the trolley will take off.

"Come on, cutie," she pleads. "I won't bite... much."

Reign slaps her arm. "Leave him alone."

She giggles and gestures toward the empty backseat. "Hop in. I'll take you wherever you want to go."

I should refuse. While part of me wants to make friends, another side is wildly attracted to Reign even though I warned myself against it. But the trolley is leaving, so I might as well accept.

"Okay." I open the back door and get in, telling them, "Thank you."

"No problem. Where are you headed?"

"Thirty, Pelham Street."

"Cool. It's Claudia, by the way," she adds, swerving back onto the road.

"Micah."

"I *know*." She stretches the word in a slow and sultry way. Only I'm not interested. "So, where are you from?"

"How did you know I'm not from around here?"

Claudia laughs. "You just told me."

I snort at myself, feeling silly to fall for that.

"Where *are* you from?" Reign asks. Her voice is like silk, smooth and skin-tingling. She watches me in the rearview mirror as she waits for my answer.

I stare at the mirror and reply honestly, "Colorado."

Claudia slows down at the traffic lights. "Wow. You came from Colorado?" She sounds surprised. She puts the windows up and turns the AC on because the night is so hot and humid.

"I think it's cool," Reign remarks, staring out the window as if she's admiring the stores along the strip. "I wouldn't mind going that far, even further," she murmurs the last part more to herself, but I hear her. I understand.

"Why Newport?" asks Claudia. She makes a left when the light switches to green.

I shrug. "Don't know, just wanted to give it a try."

"Are you usually like that?" Reign asks. Her gaze pierces mine again in the rearview. I tilt my head and watch her, trying to figure out the story behind her weary eyes.

"Something like that," I tell her. She steadies her gaze on me as if trying to unravel me. I don't look away. I can't. If anything, I like it. It's as if she's challenging me.

"So, you just get up and go spontaneously?" Claudia pipes in. "What about your parents? Are they okay with that?"

"I don't need anyone's approval. I live my own life."

As if my words have struck a chord, Reign instantly tears away and looks out the window. Headlights shine on her face from passing vehicles, and I notice the same lost expression as that day in the park. I wonder what always has her contemplating so hard.

Claudia connects her iPhone to the stereo and plays a dance song to fill the sudden silence. Without a care, she sings at the top of her lungs, drowning out the artist's voice. It's entertaining, especially since it makes Reign laugh.

She has the sexiest laugh I've ever heard. It's refreshing. It forces me to join in.

I have to snap out of this. There's no way I'll let some silly attraction overpower me. What happens once the background check clears? Will she be able to regard me the same way, or will she look at me like all the others?

In no time, Claudia turns down my street. The blue, three-story house comes into view. Slowing to a stop out front, she lowers the volume and observes the place.

"Is this it?" she asks as I exit the jeep and close the door.

I never considered how they'd perceive the house, if they came from wealth or whatnot, like some of the people I've encountered the three days I've been in Newport. On the outside, it doesn't look too bad; the paint is a tad worn—still, the rent's affordable and good enough for someone like me in a temporary situation.

I point to the double-hung windows on the third floor and say, "Yeah, I'm up there."

Following the direction of my finger, Claudia bobs her head, and her expression changes to pity as her eyes level on the exterior.

"It looks cozy," Reign chimes in sweetly. "Must be nice living on your own."

"It is," I reply fast. It would be even nicer if she wanted to spend the night.

Crap! That's why I have to get rid of these girls now. "Well, thanks again for the ride. Be careful."

"You're welcome." Claudia winks. "See ya."

"See you tomorrow." Reign waves to me.

I wait until they drive off before entering the house and hurrying upstairs. A dark, empty feeling greets me when I unlock the door and enter. I flick on the light, place my keys and cell phone on the coffee table, turn on the TV, kick off my sneakers, and head to the bathroom to shower. The second I start to linger and allow myself to feel lonely, I'll want to move again.

I need to give this place a chance. I want to meet people and learn to be happy again, at least for my gram's sake. I'm sure she'd like me to live my life without regrets. I have to try.

Stepping out of the shower, I toss the wet towel over the door and grab my shorts off the bed. After dressing, I walk to the kitchen for a water bottle.

My cell phone rings on the way to the couch. It's one of two people: my counselor in juvie or Pete from Georgetown. However, the last time I spoke to Greg, I told him I was fine and that he needed to lay off so I could breathe easily. He hasn't called me in a month, so I'm guessing it's Pete.

Sure enough, when I pick up the phone and look at the screen, it's my buddy, Pete. He's the only real friend I left back in Georgetown.

"Pete, my man, what's up?" I answer, sinking back on the couch with my legs outstretched on the coffee table.

"Not a damn thing," he says. "Man, I still can't believe you left. Feels like my game completely died when you did 'cause I can't get any girl to chill with me now."

I laugh. "Yeah, right. We both know who they were all chasing, and it sure wasn't me."

"I guess I failed to convince you to return here, huh?"

"You did," I smirk. "I'm done with Georgetown. This place isn't too bad."

"If you say so." He doesn't sound convinced. "Anyways, listen, I wanted to let you know that Ashley's been asking for you. She misses you, man. You just up and left her."

Ashley. She was one of the girls I messed around with on and off. It wasn't serious. She knew what was up.

"That's surprising," I say. "I thought she would've moved on by now."

"Man." He chuckles. I hear what sounds like traffic in the background, so I figure he's taking a cigarette break at work. "That girl's been coming around here asking if you called," he continues. "I told her you changed your number and that we don't talk. I don't like a clingy girl, so I tried to help you. Unless you want me to give her your num—"

"No!" I quickly stop him. "Don't. Tell her I got engaged. Better yet, tell her I have twins on the way."

"Oh, do you?" he jokes.

"Of course not, bro. I'm only nineteen. No way a girl's tying me down this young."

"You know you can keep it real with me, man. I won't clown you if you meet someone you want to settle down with." He laughs. "It's cool."

"Pete, come on. You know me. I'm not going to commit."

"All right. I'll stop messing with you. But like I said, Ashley's missing you badly and doesn't seem to be moving on anytime soon. So, that's just one thing to consider if you want to return."

I pause for a beat before speaking again. "There was never anything serious between us, but I might decide to visit someday."

"I hear you. Well, give me a shout whenever. I'm here if you ever want to talk."

"Thanks, Pete. I'll talk to you soon."

He's a good friend. But I haven't told him what happened in Haxtun and why I'm moving around like this. He hasn't asked, and I'm grateful for that because I'm not ready to discuss it. I'm not sure I'll share that with anyone for a long time.

SIX

Reign

THE ENTIRE drive to Claudia's house, all she does is ramble on about how hot Micah is until switching the conversation to why I won't go all the way with Nate.

"I think you should either drop him or do it. He and I aren't best friends, but he does seem serious about you, Reign. He stayed behind for you instead of going to the Caribbean. No guy gives up the opportunity to drink, party, and screw random chicks over some conservative girl with strict parents." She snorts, bumping my arm as she plops down on her bed.

A frustrated breath escapes my lips as I sink beside her. "Funny you should say that when you stayed behind, too. How come? It certainly wasn't for me."

"You know how I hate the bitches from our graduating class. Besides, they'll be back this weekend. That trip isn't long enough for all the stress we've endured in high school."

"Hmm. So true."

We stay quiet for a while, staring at her star-covered ceiling until I mutter, "I'm not ready."

"Yeah, you've been saying that." Claudia turns onto her side and eyes me intently. "I wonder..."

"Wonder what?" I ease up on my elbows.

"Maybe you don't want to go all the way with him because you don't think he's right. You've always had this fairytale idea of your first time and who it should be. And I don't think Nate falls into that description. He's nowhere near what you hope for."

"That's not true," I refute. "Nate's a great boyfriend. He treats me well, and my parents like him."

"That's not what I mean," she says, rolling her eyes.

"Well, what do you mean then?" I press.

"Even though he's a sweetie, he's too... I don't know, perfect."

I scowl. "And that's a bad thing because?"

Claudia turns and looks at me like it's clear, but I'm just too naïve to see it. "That's why you haven't told him your little issue."

The issue.

Yep. The problem I have with going into the ocean and my guilt over my sister's death.

"Because you're afraid you don't fall into his bubble of perfection," she continues. "You think he'll break up with you once he knows about that."

I steer my eyes from hers and pick at her sheets. "It's not... exactly like that."

"Whatever."

We continue to look at the ceiling. Shortly after, she breaks the silence. "Anyway, back to Micah. I want him to be my main squeeze for the rest of the summer before our trip to Miami. You think he'll go to Cooper's party this Friday?"

Somehow, her fascination with Micah makes me feel a way. "I don't know. Maybe you shouldn't do that. I work with him, and I don't want it to be awkward after you use him and toss him aside once you get bored."

She flies up and slaps my arm.

"Ow, what was that for?" I hiss, rubbing my skin as I sit up as well.

"Listen, Saint Aldridge," she grates, pointing her index at me. "I do not use guys and discard them when I'm bored. I choose not to tie myself down and date guys who feel the same way."

I slide to the edge of the bed. "Well, maybe Micah isn't one of those guys."

"Puh-lease. He's a guy, Reign. They all want the same thing."

"So you think Nate will break up with me if I keep putting off sex?"

Sighing, Claudia reaches over to her bedside table for a scrunchie to put her hair into a ponytail. "I doubt he'll break up with you for not having sex with him, at least not until he starts college. Besides, I bet his parents have already planned your wedding because Nate will need a goody-two-shoes wife once he makes it in politics."

"Shut up." I grab one of her heart-covered pillows and toss it at her, jumping from the bed before she gets the chance to hit me back. "Anyhow, I'm tired. I'll see you tomorrow."

"Yeah, right." She straightens, removes her jeans shorts and her tank top, and climbs underneath the covers in her underwear. "As if you're going to bed now, queen of insomnia," she teases as I open the door.

"You know me too well." I smile and wave before stepping outside into the hallway.

Claudia's right. I tend to stay up into the wee hours, unable to fall asleep. It's been that way since Mary drowned seven years ago.

Sometimes, when I close my eyes, I hear her cries and see her panicked face, struggling to stay above the water. That's something I don't talk about with anyone. No one mentions my sister around here, not even my parents. Still, I miss her.

I go downstairs, my steps filling the quiet house as I walk across the marble tiles and exit through the kitchen door. I always find it sad how Claudia's father and stepmom leave her behind when they take off for their annual summer vacation in Italy. All because Claudia and Eleanor don't see eye to eye.

As I stroll across the Cavallo's lawn toward my house, treacherous waves crashing ashore draw my attention. I pause to look at the full moon in the night sky, the silver-blue casting limelight across the dark ocean below. Soon, the familiar loneliness returns. I can't escape it. I don't believe I ever will.

Sighing, I glance down at the beach. The light in the workshop is still on at this hour. My ears catch the sound of a saw cutting through wood. Dad's burning the midnight oil to meet a deadline, I guess. Mary and I used to sneak out at night and watch him work, but after she died, I stopped going.

With a deep breath, I continue from the lawn and tread down the steps to the side door of my house, entering the kitchen.

Walking into the foyer, I stop and look out the window to see if Mom's car is in the driveway before I go upstairs to my room. By the looks of it, she's still at the restaurant.

I go to my room, sit on the bed, and text Natet.

Me: Are you mad?

He didn't reply to my text when I told him I couldn't be at Lucas' party. The minutes tick by, and still no response. I place the phone on my bed and peel off my clothes to shower. I'm about to walk into the bathroom when the phone rings.

"No, I'm not mad, baby," Nate says the instant I answer. "I forgot to charge my phone. It was dead the entire time I was at the party."

"Oh." I sit on the bed. "Sorry again. My mom wouldn't let me leave, and I was exhausted when we closed."

"It's no biggie. Party sucked. But you can make it up by letting me come over now."

"Now?" I slide off the bed and use the curtain to hide my body while peeking out the window, checking that his car isn't already outside my house. My stomach settles when I see that he's not there.

"Yeah, now," he laughs. "You can let me in through the side door and sneak me to your room."

He's never done that before. The only time he's been to my house is to have dinner with my parents. We've never been alone here, and he's never been in my room.

"Um, my dad's still up," I tell him.

"Okay, so text me when he goes to bed."

I bite my nails. "My mom isn't home yet. She's still at the restaurant."

"Same goes for her, too." He scoffs. "Come on, Reign. I want to see you tonight and kiss your lips before I go to bed."

Sighing, I move my phone away from my ear and check the time. It's already eleven-thirty. I don't know if I should accept and risk getting caught by either of my parents or end up sleeping with Nate when I don't want to. Gosh, he makes me feel so pressured sometimes. That must be the real reason why he wants to come over. Sneaking into my room has never been a topic before.

"Babe?" he prods.

I know he'll be mad, but I'm uncomfortable. I swallow hard before telling him, "Sorry. I can't."

The line falls silent until he says in a low and frustrated tone, "Okay. Maybe some other time when you're cool with it."

"Don't be mad." I can't stand the dread in my heart that I feel when someone's mad at me. It's pathetic.

"I'm not. Look, I'm tired after all. We'll talk tomorrow."

And without waiting for me to say another word, he hangs up.

SEVEN

Micah

IT RAINED most of Tuesday morning. When the dark clouds move away and allow the sun to peek out again, I bring the chairs back on the deck and wipe off the tables.

I glimpse Reign as I turn to head back inside. She's leaning against the wall, staring into space. I stand there and study her. Like that day at the park, she appears lost in thought and troubled, as if bricks are on her shoulders.

Dammit. I should walk away. Mind my own business. But I can't. Something else takes over, making me move towards her. Before I can backtrack, I hear myself ask, "You okay?"

Light emphasizes her features so much that she almost looks unreal. Her gorgeous hazel eyes are brighter than ever, and at the same time, they seem so sad. My stomach clenches. I want to make her laugh as she did last night.

Reign catches her breath before she answers, "Yeah." Still holding my gaze, she sighs and says softly, "No."

"Want to talk about it?" I offer without thinking.

She drops her eyes and looks over the wooden railing at the water below. I feel as if I've made her uncomfortable. After all, we don't know each other.

"I'm sorry. I'll leave you—"

"It's just," she stops me before I walk away, "I feel like I should do so much more. Have you ever felt that way? But there are too many things holding you back?"

"Yeah," I say, remembering when I thought doing more meant stepping out of my comfort zone. That feeling landed me in trouble.

I edge closer to her. "So, what is it you want to do? And what's keeping you from doing it?" I swiftly retract. "Sorry, I probably shouldn't have asked. I mean, we've been co-workers for just a day."

"Where do you want to go next?" she asks, ignoring what I said.

I stare into her eyes, smiling as I answer playfully, "Why? You want to come with me?"

"You wish," she quips. A nervous laugh escapes her lips. She tucks a loose strand behind her ear as if she's shy all of a sudden.

I grin, taking a second to regard her beauty before telling her, "I haven't decided where to go next."

Narrowing her eyes, Reign starts to do that thing again where she's trying to read me. "But my mom only hired you for summer," she says. "You should start looking for another job if you want to stick around after that."

43

"Oh, I get it," I say, folding my arms and winking at her. "You want me to stay in Newport, huh? That's why you were asking about where I'm going next."

She snorts and approaches the dark railing, resting her elbows on the wood as she turns her back to the water to look at me, still smiling. "I was only curious. I think it's cool how you're so young, yet you've been traveling with no cares in the world."

I put my hands in my pockets and move to the railing to stand beside her. "You sound jealous," I tease.

"Kind of," she admits, never taking that gorgeous smile off her face. "How come you didn't go to New York?"

I'm curious now. "Why New York?"

She shrugs. "Everyone I know goes to New York or California, or they leave the country altogether."

I bob my head, figuring her out. "Your mom told me you want to travel."

She twists a bit to observe the sailboats in the distance. "I do, but... it's hard."

I'm beyond intrigued and becoming aware that I'm lessening the distance between us. I want to keep talking. I want to learn everything about this girl, and I also want our hands to brush.

I need to feel her touch again.

"Sounds like you're looking for an adventure," I assume, continuing our conversation.

Her lips turn down, and she stares at her fingers. Chipping at her already worn purple nail polish, she replies in a sigh, "Something like that."

Silence sweeps in and lingers over us like a fog.

Reign finally looks up and peers at the sailboats in the harbor.

The restaurant is in a great spot, with Newport Bridge and a few eye-catching islands in the distance. The deck is built over the water so customers can dine on the sea while basking in their surroundings' natural beauty. It's the perfect setting for dates.

Why am I thinking like this, all romantic and shit?

"Why are you two standing around?" I zap out of it at Mrs. Aldridge's sharp voice. "Customers are starting to show up."

Reign slips away first and treads past her mom. I follow, noting a questioning look in Mrs. Aldridge's eyes as I walk by her. I make a mental note not to approach Reign when she's by herself again. Not when her mom's lurking nearby.

A few hours before closing, I step out back to take a break, staring up at the starry sky as I visualize Reign's beautiful face in each of them looking down on me. Man, I'm seriously losing it over this girl.

"Hey."

Startled, I turn around fast. Aislin has an eyebrow raised and a cigarette between her fingers.

"What?" I ask.

"Been asking if you got a light?"

I shake my head. "No. That's bad for you, anyway."

She sucks her teeth and saunters to the brick wall to lean against it. "That's what everybody tells me. But it's my life, and it's now or never. I won't live forever. I want to live while I'm alive."

Laughter bursts out of me. "Did you just quote Bon Jovi?"

Aislin turns her head toward me and shrugs, a smile playing at the corner of her mouth. Sticking the cigarette back into the box, she slips it into her pocket and glances up at the stars.

It hits me that we haven't spoken much since yesterday. "How long have you been at *Captain's Choice*?"

"Almost a year now," she replies, still looking up.

"You from Newport?"

She snorts. "I'm from all over Rhode Island."

"Okay..."

Meeting my gaze, she clarifies, "I was in several foster homes before I turned eighteen. I moved to Newport last year."

I nod, understanding. "So, what is it with you and Reign's boyfriend?"

Irritation floods her eyes. "He's fake."

"Ouch."

"Yeah, except she's too nice to see it. That moron flirts with other girls when he goes to parties without her. Reign's too good for him."

What a jerk. Reign's not even my girlfriend, yet she makes me feel uninterested in others. Is this guy blind?

"Anyway." Aislin pushes off the wall and slants to head back inside. "I'm taking off. You want a ride?"

"No, I'm good. I'll catch the trolley."

She shrugs. "Suit yourself. See you tomorrow." She turns to leave.

Going back inside, I change clothes and hurry out of the restaurant to catch the trolley. I realize it isn't here when I reach the stop, so I sit on the bench to wait. A minute later, a silver Corolla pulls up next to me. It's Reign.

"Hey, hop in. I'll drive you home."

I want to get in her car so badly. Still, I fight the urge. "That's okay. Don't want to make this a habit."

"How is it a habit when I'm the one offering this time and not Claudia?"

"Still is," I smirk, not getting up from the bench.

Reign eyes me with a pinch between her brows. "Did my mom give you a warning?"

"Warning?" I ask in my confusion.

"She does it whenever a guy my age starts working at the restaurant. I'm sorry. It must have made you uncomfortable."

I laugh nervously. "Uh, actually, she didn't."

"Oh." Her sweet smile reappears. "Well, expect it to happen soon. Until then, hop in. I'm going that way."

The trolley's approaching now. All I have to do is say no and get on it. What happened to hands-off? What happened to staying away from the boss's daughter?

Screw that. This girl is too damn enticing.

I open the passenger door and hop in, grinning too much.

"Nice car, by the way," I say as I buckle my seatbelt.

"Thanks." She takes off.

The drive is relatively quiet. As we draw close to the left turn for my street, I realize I don't want to get out of the car yet. I want to spend more time talking to Reign and learn more about whatever is holding her back.

47

I shut my eyes and mentally smack myself for disregarding my warning. Before I can give more thought to it, I ask, "Want to hang out a bit? I mean, if you're not too tired."

She looks at me briefly and sets her eyes back on the road. I figure I've crossed a line this time, but to my surprise, she says, "Sure. I want to check out this waterfront lounge and catch the last part of a performance. Want to go?"

Hell yeah! Her invitation thrills me since it's too hard to stay away. It doesn't matter where—a Celine Dion concert, to watch a chick flick, whatever—damn right, I'm going with her.

"Yeah," I reply. "Take me wherever."

Smiling, she drives past my street. I cannot wait to see how this night unfolds.

EIGHT

Reign

I HAVE NO IDEA WHY, but I was relieved when Micah asked if I wanted to hang out. Honestly, I find it refreshing to be around someone who isn't from Newport—someone who doesn't know me. Someone free.

The indie band has already finished their performance by the time we arrive. Since it's late and there's not much to do on a Tuesday night, I suggest we drive to the pier and hang out for a while.

I park nearby and lead Micah to where the boats are, pointing out Aster—the one my dad built for Mary and me.

The dock is chained off, so we can't get a closer look. We stroll over to a bench and sit down.

"That's cool," he says. "You guys must have a lot of fun with that baby."

Aster is sentimental to me, and Micah's a stranger. Yet I feel so relaxed around him that I almost want to spill everything. Almost. "We don't go out on it anymore. Long story," I add when he wrinkles his brows.

"And I get that it's not one we're going to discuss," he replies, understanding. He looks behind at the boat and asks, "Your dad builds them for a living?"

"No." I peer down and pick at my jeans, muttering, "He doesn't anymore."

"What does he do now?"

As I look up, he returns his gaze to meet mine. Surprisingly, a chill runs down my spine, and I fight to catch my breath to answer. "He's still building stuff. Only he makes things like storage benches, chests, bookcases."

"That's still crafty. But how come your dad doesn't build boats anymore?"

"He—" I stop myself from going further, saying instead, "That's another long story."

His mouth curves into a sympathetic smile that arouses a strange tingling sensation in my tummy. I can't keep myself from smiling, too.

I blink out of it and change the subject. "Um, how do you like Newport so far? When did you come here, anyway?"

"Last Friday. It's okay so far; nothing too exciting."

"So you're looking for excitement?"

He arches over and clasps his hands, surveying me with a sly grin. "That depends. Are you up for exciting me?"

I dip my head back in a short laugh. "Do you always make these flirtatious remarks with your co-workers?"

Straightening, he creases his forehead and looks at me appalled. "What flirtatious remarks? Relax, sweetness. This is how I am."

"Okay, whatever you say, Micah."

He glances at the pub across from the pier. They're turning their lights off. I look at my phone and see it's approaching midnight. But I don't want to head home just yet.

"How about I show you around on Sunday since we open later that day?" I'm not sure why I offer, but I like the sound of giving him a tour of Newport, something to help him feel at home here.

"That'll be great," he says with a delighted grin.

We fall silent until curiosity sneaks up on me again. "Are you ever going back to Colorado? What about your family?"

"It's a long story," he replies, using my own words. "How old is that boat?" He doesn't seem to want to talk about himself or his family either.

Taking a moment, I think back to when Dad started working on Aster. "It's about eight years old."

Mary died only a year after Dad finished it. Of course, I don't tell Micah that part or mention anything about having a dead sister.

He whistles. "And it's just been sitting there? Come on. You have to take it out sometime."

The intimate topic makes me uneasy. "I'm feeling hungry. Want a late-night snack?" I divert. "There's a spot down the street that opens late."

Micah's gaze lingers on me for a beat before he says, "Sure. I'll buy."

We ease up from the bench at the same time. Our hands graze. The brief touch tickles my skin, and I fear I'll break out in goosebumps.

I'm baffled by my silly reaction. He's just another guy who works for my mother. I've bumped into John and others countless times at the restaurant but never felt the same intensity.

It's weird. I don't remember ever experiencing this with Nate. What's even stranger is that I only now remember my boyfriend. Geez!

Looking up at Micah's face, he wrenches away from my eyes and reaches his hand behind his neck. He feels that strangeness, too. I can tell.

I should put distance between us. I have to. Fast.

"Um, actually, you want to call it a night? I feel sleepy suddenly," I lie. I'm not sleepy at all. I could go jogging right this instant. That's how awake and energetic the buzzing between us makes me feel.

"Yeah, me too," he replies, appearing slightly upset as he shoves his hands in his jeans pockets and combs the ground for something only he can pick out in the dark. Oh yeah, it's awkward between us.

I start moving first. Micah falls in stride behind me as his footsteps mimic mine across the boardwalk.

We return to my car and hop in, not uttering another word. I drive him home and take off the second he gets out. I don't wait until he enters the apartment.

The brush of our hands plays in my head, along with the odd sensation I felt. Both puzzle me until I reach my house and park behind Mom's SUV.

Is it normal for a girl to chill with a guy who isn't her boyfriend late at night? No. That can't be right in the name of relationships. Then again, didn't I offer to show him around Newport? It's a friendly gesture as his co-worker. That's all. I should relax.

I walk into the house, hearing someone rifling around in the kitchen. I enter the arched doorway to find my dad, dressed for bed in his PJs, going through the cabinets.

"What are you looking for, Dad?" I ask, stepping across the hardwood floor over to the island.

He peers back at me briefly and continues searching. "I think your mom hid those hostess ding dongs from me, that sneaky woman. She wants them all for herself when I'm the one who bought them in the first place."

I chuckle. "Well, why don't you just ask her?"

Finally giving up, he settles for a box of saltines instead and gets a bottle of cranberry juice from the fridge, pouring two glasses. "She's relaxing in the tub, and I know she won't tell me even if I ask."

He puts the rest of the juice away and hands me one of the glasses. "Here you go, honey."

I take it from him. "Thanks, Dad."

He bites down on a saltine. I'm about to sip when he says coolly, "Mom's worried about my health."

"Should we be?" I ask, concern cutting through my voice.

Dad waves me off. "Don't you get all sappy on me. I'm fine." He wrinkles his thick, dark brows, asking, "Did you and Claudia hang out after work?"

"Ye-yes," I fumble my reply. Why am I lying?

He eyes me for a passing second, then drops his eyes to the granite and drinks his juice. He knows I lied. I'm not good at it.

Dad picks up the box of crackers and glass, walks around the island, and kisses me on the forehead. "I'm going to head up to bed. You do the same."

"Okay," I say as he leaves the kitchen. "Oh, did you finish that project you worked on late last night?"

He stops in the doorway and looks at me sideways. "Not yet. But you mind staying out of the workshop until I finish?"

That makes me curious, even though I haven't been going in there. "How come?"

"You'll know soon enough," he says with a smile. "Just stay out for now."

I nod.

"Well, goodnight, honey."

"Night, Dad."

Shortly after finishing my juice, I go to my room and shower before bed. I haul on my blue sleeveless nightshirt and climb under the covers, lying there in the dark, unable to fall asleep. I can't stop thinking about that touch and Micah's sexy smile.

Buzzing on the table jolts me out of it. I reach for my phone and see a text from Nate. It makes me feel guilty for thinking about another guy.

Nate: Hey, babe. I missed you today.

Me: Hey, what are you still doing up?
Partying?

Nate: you know I hate partying without you.

I twist my mouth, not believing him.

Me: So you say.

**Nate: I'm up thinking about you, babe.
I miss you. Ask your mom for the day
off tomorrow so we can hang out.**

I consider his request. Time together will do us good. Before we know it, summer will be over, and it'll be even harder to see each other when Nate goes off to Brown University in Providence and I'll be at URI in South Kingstown.

I can't just spend the entire summer working and neglecting my boyfriend. Mom will have to understand.

Nate: Babe?

Me: OK, I will.

Nate: Awesome! I can't wait to see you.

Me: Yeah, me either. I miss hanging out with you.

**Nate: Well, I'm dozing off, babe.
Call me tomorrow, and I'll pick you up.
We'll chill at our special place.**

Me: OK, see you tomorrow. Night, babe.

Nate: Night. Dream about me.

Me: I will once I fall asleep.

Nate: All right. Well, I'll dream about you. Love you.

He's been saying that to me. Sadly, I can't say it back, even in text.

Adore you.

As my eyes flutter open from the sunlight pouring into the room, I spring out of bed, put on my pink robe, and hasten downstairs to catch Mom before she leaves for the restaurant.

Dad's at the table having breakfast and reading the newspaper while Mom's munching on croissants and skimming through papers on the island. She turns and regards my appearance as I enter the kitchen.

With a short wave, she asks, "Why aren't you dressed? Honey, we open in two hours."

I lean against the island beside her and reply in a fake groggy tone, "I'm not feeling so good. Can I take the day off?"

Mom scoffs and drops the half-eaten croissant on the plate to place her hands on her hips. "You just started helping out again this week, Reign. We're already down two people. I don't want my customers complaining that our service has gotten slow and lose even more of them."

"She can have one day, Sophia. Come on," Dad comes to my rescue. He reaches over and gently touches her arm. "You get going. It's all right if she misses a day. Our daughter is human, too."

Looking at him, Mom relaxes her face. She's unable to stifle back her smile. Gosh, they're so in love. She brushes her shoulder-length hair—a shade lighter than the cool brown she was rocking a week ago—behind her ears before kissing Dad on the cheek.

"You know, if she were working for some other business, she wouldn't have the luxury of taking off whenever she wanted."

"I know that, Mom. I don't feel like it today," I mumble, sitting at the table.

She studies me with a questioning look. "Don't feel like it or don't feel good? Which is it?"

I innocently bounce my gaze between them, muttering, "I don't... feel good."

Mom presses her lips together, shakes her head, and returns to the island to finish her croissant.

Picking up her coffee mug, she turns to Dad and gives him another kiss. "I'll see you later, dear." Walking over to me, she exhales before brushing back my messy strands to peck my forehead. "See you later."

"Bye, Mom. Thank you."

She exits the kitchen, grabbing her keys and handbag from the table by the stairs before leaving the front door.

I pick up a buttery croissant from the platter in the middle of the table and pour some orange juice.

Dad sets the newspaper down next to his plate. He angles his head to one side and eyes me knowingly. "So, what do you have planned that you don't want to go to the restaurant today?"

"Nothing." I smile before helping myself to another croissant.

"Hmm." He reaches over and squeezes my shoulder. Then he rises from the table. "I'm going into town to deliver some things. You be good."

"Aren't I always? By the way, how's business going?"

"Good. Business is good." He doesn't elaborate. Turning to leave, he says, "Tell Nate I say hi."

Dad doesn't wait for me to deny it. He hurries out the front door.

After eating, I quickly wash the dishes, go to my room, shower, blow-dry my hair, dress in shorts and a sleeveless top, and call Nate to pick me up.

Our special place is out by the rocks on Ocean Drive, not too far from where he lives. Only, it doesn't look so special when we hop out of his car, walk down the beach, and I see his friends.

Slowing down, I say quietly, "I thought it was just going to be us."

Nate nudges my arm. "Come on, babe. Don't be so anti-social." He walks off, and I follow behind, silently seething.

Lucas, Ryan, and Kimberly appear buzzed already. Kimberly flashes me a frown when she sees me over Nate's shoulder.

"Hey, peeps," Nate says as we reach them.

"Hey. So, what's on the agenda for today?" Lucas asks, handing him a Budweiser.

"I thought we could go out on my dad's boat after hanging out here," Nate replies.

My stomach coils. He knows I don't do boats, and even if he doesn't understand why, he should at least consider my feelings.

"Cool," Ryan raves, lowering to pick up another beer from the cooler as he finishes the one in his hand.

Kimberly stares down her nose at me as the boys chat. She's wearing an itty-bitty red bikini with a bandeau top that barely covers her huge boobs.

Flipping her long blonde hair off her shoulders, she jogs over to the water, splashing it on herself before diving under. Her thong doesn't leave much to the imagination. She probably thinks I'm lame, coming to the beach without a bathing suit.

Whatever. I never planned on going swimming.

I look back at the boys and catch Nate ogling Kimberly. He glances at me, his guilty face burning red, and half-smiles as if I didn't just see him lusting for her ass.

Breaking away from the guys, he hands me a beer. "Here you go, babe."

I shake my head. "I'm good."

My response causes him to frown. "What's up?"

"Nothing," I reply.

He shrugs me off and rejoins the guys, placing the beer back inside the cooler as they resume their conversation.

So much for wanting to hang out with me alone.

Nate spends the time talking with his friends and paying me no attention. I sit by Kimberly as she sunbathes on the sand. When I try to have a conversation with her, she acts uninterested.

"How was your first semester at Brown?" I ask her. "Must be nice to live and study in the city."

She keeps her eyes covered with her sunglasses and lets out an exasperated sigh, answering flatly, "It's all right."

All I know about her is that her father is the hospitality manager at Newport Harbor Hotel and that he also went to Brown University. There's the rumor— well, Claudia told me—that she and Ryan hooked up a couple of times.

I'm sure that's why she's always hanging around the guys even though she's a year older than us. I don't think Ryan wants anything serious because he flirts with other girls around her when they go to parties.

Kimberly seems annoyed with my presence, but I have nothing to do but wait until Nate gets bored and decides to leave, which takes him another hour. They discuss heading to Nate's house to take his dad's boat out. That's a big no-no.

"Let's go, babe," he says, draping his arm around me as he leads me up the beach.

The others follow behind.

"Nate, can we skip the boat for another time?" I ask in a whisper so his friends don't hear.

He scrunches up his face. "Why?"

"You know why," I say. "I don't like boats."

Twisting his mouth, he huffs an annoyed breath, not saying anything until we reach his car. "All right, we'll go another time."

I pause at the passenger side door. "Really? Is it okay?"

He smiles, edges closer, and kisses me softly on the lips. "Of course, it's fine. I won't force you to go out on the boat and make it miserable for everyone else."

He slips away and walks over to his friends to tell them there's a change of plans. Kimberly shoots me a death glare.

I couldn't care less. Nate's reply bothers me more—the irritation in his words. He's more concerned about me ruining the day for his friends. His remark is new.

Sighing, I open the door and get in as he walks back. Sliding in behind the steering wheel, Nate backs off the grass and pulls out onto the main road.

"Let's go back to your house and hang out," he suggests.

I don't voice my apprehension. I nod.

NINE

Micah

"GREEK SALAD and French onion soup," John mutters behind me when an old couple enters the restaurant.

I look at him while sliding off the bar stool. "I'm guessing they're regulars who always get the same thing."

A smug look masks his face as he wipes off the glasses. "Yep, even though they're waiting at the door, they'll pick the table by the window."

I walk over to the couple and tell them to choose a table. Sure enough, they choose the one by the window.

"Something to drink while you're looking through the menu?"

"Oh, we can order now," the husband informs me.

"Are you new? I haven't seen you here before," says the wife. As I direct my attention to her, my stomach tightens when I gaze into her sharp emerald eyes.

In a flash, I see Grams looking back at me. My hands start to shake. The organ in my chest starts to pound harder. I can't get a hold of myself. I need a minute—a moment to chill out.

A hand at my back jolts me out of it. Looking to my left, I find Aislin taking their orders. She finishes and pulls me along with her from the table.

"Take a break," she whispers before going to the bar to put in their order.

I glance at the old couple, staring at me with confusion. Feeling awkward, I turn away and walk outside, rubbing my temples while I lean against the wall. I haven't had a moment like that in a few days. I have to get a grip on my emotions. And while I'm beating myself up, I hate that Reign isn't at work today. Her beauty is the distraction I need.

The door opens, and Aislin strides over to me. She rests one hand on the wall and drops the other on her hip, asking, "You okay?"

"Yeah," I say, flicking from her searching gaze.

She sniffs. "Uh, you froze in there. Are you sick or something?"

I look at her and reply, "I'm fine. Just didn't get a good night's sleep."

Eyes still studying my appearance, she says, "Take a few more minutes before you return inside. It's slow in there, anyway." Then she turns and heads for the door.

"Thanks," I mutter before she slips inside.

"Don't mention it."

I linger in place a bit longer, then go back into the restaurant. A group of girls enter. They're hot, and their sweet perfumes engulf me as I lead them to a table on the deck. But amidst their flirty giggles and naughty eye contact, my mind drifts to Reign. I wonder why she's not working and what she's doing. I wish she were here today.

TEN

Reign

IN NO TIME, Nate pulls up to my house. Getting out of the car, he hurries around and picks me up into his arms, carrying me the rest of the way. The gesture makes me laugh, and my sulkiness from earlier disappears.

"Are you hungry?" I ask when he settles me back on my feet, and we step into my house.

He wraps his arms around me. Brushing his lips lightly against my left ear, he whispers sweetly, "I'm hungry. Hungry for you."

Giggling nervously, I pry myself out of his embrace and lead him into the living room. "How about we watch a movie instead?"

He nods and strides over with me, looking slightly disappointed as we sit on the couch.

Within minutes of starting the romantic comedy, Nate nuzzles up to me and starts kissing my neck. He places his hand on my stomach and inches even closer, so much so that he manages to slide me down on my back, gently running his fingers down to the hem of my blouse. He sticks his hand underneath and traces the area around my belly button. Uneasy, I shift away, press my palm against his chest, and ease him back.

Nate ignores my hint and drives in again, reaching under my blouse to unclasp my bra. Utterly surprised by his bold attempt, I push him off and spring from the couch, fixing myself immediately.

"Geez." He shoots up, his brown eyes darkened by anger I've never seen before. He makes me feel like the worst girlfriend in the world right now.

Maybe I am.

"What's wrong, Reign? Why don't you want to be with me?" His tone is sharp, biting.

I back up a few steps. "I told you I'm not ready."

"What the hell!" he snaps, making me shudder. It's the first time he's yelled at me. "We've been dating for almost three months, so I'm sure you've realized by now that I care about you a lot." He runs his hand through his tousled blond hair. "Like, what the fuck! Just tell me what the problem is 'cause I don't get it."

Pissed at his reaction, I ball my fists and snap back at him. "Why does it have to be a problem because I'm not ready for sex? If you truly care about me, I'm sure you can wait for—"

"That's just it," he cuts me off. "It feels like it'll never happen." He waves his hands about, adding, "There's always an excuse with you."

My eyes sting from the surge of tears, but they don't fall. I maintain my composure as I ask, "Why are you so mad at me over that?" I look down at my bare feet on the hardwood floor.

Nate releases a long breath and closes the distance between us, touching my arm. "Babe," he says in a calmer tone. "I only want us to be closer. I think it's great that you saved yourself all this time. But I feel like you don't think *I* deserve it. That I don't deserve you."

Looking up to meet his gaze, I shake my head and drape my arms around his neck. "That's not true. It's just me... I'm nervous about it, that's all."

He gently eases me away to look at my face as he says, "There's no need to be. We feel the same way about each other, so it'll be great."

Nate makes it sound like it would be his first time, too. He's no virgin. He lost his back in the eighth grade to some random girl in one of his classes. But that doesn't matter. He's with me now, and like Claudia says, guys have needs.

I breathe in and out, then manage a smile. "Okay."

A broad grin spreads across his face. He strokes my cheek and takes my hand, leading me to the stairs. I haul him back, laughing nervously. "Not now. Sunday, after I leave work."

His smile falters before he pulls me into his arms, whispering at my neck, "All right. I'll make it special for you, babe. I promise."

I relax in his arms and rest my head on his shoulder. Pressing my eyes shut, I tell myself repeatedly that I'm making the right decision.

Dad and I have dinner together while Mom is still at the restaurant. He spoke to her on the phone earlier while I was cooking, his voice low and almost inaudible, as if he didn't want me to hear.

Dad doesn't make any eye contact. We're eating in silence, and I have all these thoughts running through my head. I don't ask what's going on. I don't want to be rude.

Mary was never rude. She knew to mind her business.

I start up the usual dinner table conversation. "How was your day?"

"Hmm? Oh, it was good. How was yours?" he asks, helping himself to more lasagna.

I swallow what's in my mouth. "It was good."

Silence engulfs us again until dinner ends. I arrange the plates in the dishwasher and enter the living room, where Dad's watching a movie on the couch. He gestures me over.

"It's one of our favorites," he says, "*The Gold Rush*."

He's in the same spot where Nate felt me up earlier. An awkward feeling takes hold of my stomach, and I can't move out of the doorway, fearing I might throw up dinner.

"I'm going for a walk," I tell him instead.

"Now?" Dad glances at his watch and looks back at me with a pinch between his brows. "It's almost ten."

"I'll go down the street and come right back. I barely got any exercise in today."

"Oh...well." He delays in thought, then says, "All right, but don't stay out too late."

I'm out the door immediately, leaving my car behind as I walk past Claudia's house, pacing down the street and out of the neighborhood even though I said I'd be right back.

It's happening again. The lonely feeling is creeping up on me.

All I'm thinking about is Mary. I want to see her calm face. I would love to hear her voice again. But all I hear are her panicked screams.

My steps quicken into a jog, and I run for several minutes before I find myself at the beach.

Stopping to catch my breath, I remove my shoes and walk to the sand, collapsing on the ground. I bring my knees to my chest, lock my arms around them, and sit still, staring at the dark ocean.

Voices echo all around me as couples stroll up and down the beach. Hand in hand, smiling, laughing together, they all seem utterly happy. No one notices me, or they choose not to. No one sees the lonely girl on the sand, fighting back the tears, overcome by guilt.

I let my sister drown. I let her die.

After a while, I draw in the immense pain and stabilize it back in my heart. When it's locked away deep enough to carry me through the rest of the night, I stand, brush sand off my clothes, and start back up the beach.

I speed-walk home, noticing Mom's car in the driveway. Entering the house, I see my parents sitting in the dark, snuggled up on the couch, the black and white lights of the movie flashing across their faces. They look over at me as I start for the stairs.

"You okay, honey?" Mom calls out.

My throat feels like a desert and burns from all the internal fighting on the beach. I swallow before answering, "I'm fine." Then I continue upstairs to avoid her leaving the living room to check on me.

I slip into my room and shut the door. Without turning on the light, I peel out of my clothes and hop in the shower, washing off grains of sand.

Shoulders feeling heavy, I crawl into bed naked with damp hair and pull the covers over me, remembering that I haven't spoken to my best friend all day. That's odd for us.

I grab my jeans shorts off the floor and pull my phone out of the pocket. I have two missed calls and three text messages. All are from Nate, telling me to come to Ryan's party tomorrow night after work and that I must wear a bikini even if I don't want to go into the pool. His messages feel demanding, but I let them slide. I want to be a good girlfriend. I want us to have a fun summer, and I want us to work.

That's all I want. Right?

ELEVEN

Micah

"WANT TO COME with us to a party?" Claudia asks me as I walk out of the restaurant to head home.

Slowing down, I massage my neck while considering whether I should. "Uh, I don't know." I'm hesitant about hanging out at a party with so many strangers. Even if I'm interested in making friends, there are certain things I don't want to join in on.

Claudia leans her head to one side and puts on the puppy look. "Please come. It'll be fun." She glances over her shoulder at Reign, standing by the passenger door of the jeep. "Won't it?"

Reign looks at me and gnaws at her bottom lip, unsure whether she should help her friend lure me into going. She chips at her nail polish and scowls, bouncing her gaze from Claudia to me. "Um, I guess it'll be fun."

There's still something off about her demeanor. She's been like that all day. I wonder what's up.

"See?" Claudia chirps, her eyes bright with excitement. "We *both* want you to come."

Honestly, I'm not ready for the night to end. Like Wednesday, I want to hang out with Reign more, even if her friend is around. And Claudia's all right, I guess.

"Come on, Micah," she begs. "It's Friday."

"Sure," I concede.

We pile into the jeep and take off from the restaurant, arriving at a waterfront property by Easton's Beach several minutes later.

Claudia drives through the black wrought-iron gates and parks alongside the many expensive cars.

She hops out first. Reign sighs before getting out as well. I follow them to the stone path, which loops around to the back of the house and steps that continue to the beach.

The second I spot the crowd, I regret coming.

Most of the guys seem wasted, spraying beer all over the girls and pushing them into the pool. I didn't know it was going to be a late-night pool party.

Claudia quickly hauls off her cover-up and reveals her burgundy bikini with triangle strings tied around her neck. She doesn't look half bad, but I'm more interested in seeing what Reign has on underneath.

She doesn't take off her t-shirt or slide out of her shorts. She's just playing with her pockets and rocking back and forth in her flip-flops, appearing shy. I wonder why she even bothered to come when it's obvious she doesn't like parties.

My stomach churns as her cocky boyfriend pops out of the crowd, and I realize she forced herself to come because of him—the things girls do for their so-called love.

"Hey, babe!" he yells over the loud music, smothering her lips with his mouth the moment he reaches her. His hands glide over her arms as he pushes his body against hers. I cringe at his roughness.

To make things worse, he tugs at her t-shirt, trying to remove it. She politely moves his hands.

"Come on, let's see it!" he urges, a perverted grin masking his face.

What is she doing with this prick?

I edge forward to assure her she doesn't have to do anything that makes her uncomfortable. Before I can, Claudia hooks her arm around mine and wrenches me away, leading me toward the sliding doors.

"Let's get some drinks," she says.

I glance back at Reign, wondering if she needs help. She finally gives in, hauls her top over her head, and takes off her shorts, showing off a blue one-piece bathing suit that emphasizes her curvy frame. I can't help but gawk.

Damn! She's sexy.

Nate's scrunched-up expression as he eyes her from the chest down tells me he's not as impressed as I am.

Are you kidding me? Talk about unappreciative.

The music gets louder as we move past the DJ, so I can't hear what he says to her. From the look on Reign's face, it's obvious he must have hurt her feelings.

Claudia leads me through the doors and into the living room. We stroll down a red-painted passage, passing drunk couples making out in every corner until we reach the kitchen.

She opens the fridge and glances over her shoulder at me. "Budweiser, Coors Light, or Heineken?"

"Coke," I tell her.

She snorts. "It's Friday night. Live a little."

I ignore her remark. "Coke's fine. Thanks."

Reaching inside, she pulls out a can for me and a Budweiser for herself. Then she walks over to the island and gestures for us to sit on the stools.

"Maybe you shouldn't be drinking," I advise after taking the soda from her. "I mean, you're driving Reign home."

Narrowing her eyes to slits, she watches me keenly over her beer. "Are you worried about her or me?"

"Both." I rest my elbow on the island's marble surface.

A flirty grin stretches her lips as she sets the bottle down. "So, Micah, you got a girlfriend back in Colorado or... anywhere?"

I drink before answering, "No."

"Would you like one?" She slowly brings the bottle to her lips and winks at me as she chugs it.

"Hey." I reach over and touch her hand. "Slow down, and no, I'm too busy."

She licks her lips and holds the bottle still. "Oh, I see. You're not looking for any attachments."

Two girls sashay into the kitchen, and one opens the fridge to get a beer. The other flashes Claudia a dirty look and whispers something to her friend holding the bottles. She glances at us, and they giggle as they walk out.

"What was that about?" I ask. "You know them?"

Her smile fades. "Yeah. Kimberly, the blonde, is dating my ex now."

"So why are we even at this party?"

"Mutual friends. Anyway." She shifts on the stool and faces me. "Back to you and me."

I lift a brow. "You and me?"

Her pearly whites go on display with the sly smile. She places her hand on my thigh and gently runs her index finger back and forth. "About that no attachment thing. I agree with it."

Looking at her closely, Claudia *is* beautiful. And if this were Illinois, where I was sleeping with a different girl every other week to suppress my guilt, she'd be the kind of girl I'd have fun with and move on. But my mind keeps drifting to Reign, the girl with a boyfriend.

Suddenly, I'm over the party and want to leave. I ease Claudia's hand away and apologize as I stand. "Sorry, but I have to go. As I've said, it's been a long day, and I'm tired."

"Wait." She hops off the stool. Edging closer to me, she rests her hand on my chest and dips her head back as if she wants me to kiss her, or rather, like she's going to reach up and take it. After all, she seems like the kind of girl to take charge.

"Why don't I drive you home, and we can hang out," she offers.

"Listen, Claudia, you seem like a nice girl, but I can't. Sorry." I move her hand and walk out of the kitchen. I cross the living room, ignoring the gyrating and make-out sessions. I almost expect Claudia to follow me out the front door. She doesn't.

The music fades as I walk down the stone entrance toward the front gates. Hearing waves crashing, I make a U-turn to check out the water before heading home. It's not too far from my house, anyway.

Taking off my sneakers, I hold them in one hand and stride barefoot in the sand down the beach until I can't hear any music or loud voices from the house.

It's nice being alone with nothing but the sound of the ocean. It drowns out everything. Not even my memories interrupt the moment of peace.

I walk to the shoreline and pause, staring at the dark ocean while water rushes to my feet, cooling them.

After some time passes, I turn to head back, noticing someone coming toward me—a girl. The blanket of night shields her appearance until she's closer, and I recognize the long hair blowing in the breeze and the protective way she hugs herself.

Reign.

She's wearing her t-shirt and shorts again. "Hey," she says with a slight curve of her lips as she reaches me.

"Hey."

"You don't like parties?" she asks, motioning back at the house.

"Not really. You don't either, huh?"

She unfolds her arms and tucks her hair behind her ears. Facing the ocean, she looks down at her toes digging into the sand and watches as water washes her tiny feet. I notice she flinches a tad when it touches her.

"No," she finally breathes out. "I just came 'cause Nate wanted me to. And Claudia wanted to hang out with you."

Ignoring the last part, I step closer to her. "What would you like to do instead?"

She tilts her head back and peers up at the full moon, its luminous light shining down on the black ocean. She stays quiet for a beat before saying, "I'd love to go swimming."

I lean forward to study her face. Once again, she's in deep thought.

"Let's go then," I say, tossing my sneakers into the sand and hauling my shirt over my head. Reign widens her eyes in astonishment, watching me take off my jeans.

"What?" she mutters.

"Coming?" I urge, excited about rushing into the ocean with her. At night. Alone. We'll probably be touching, and that's the best part.

My smile fades as she shakes her head and backs up. I stop walking into the water the moment I recognize the expression on her face.

She's afraid.

"I-I can't," she says, her voice a near whisper.

I crumple my brows. "You just said you'd love to go swimming. So let's go—"

"I didn't mean now."

"Oh... Okay." She has me baffled.

Reign looks straight into my eyes. I so want to disentangle that mind of hers.

When her gaze drifts down to my chest and lingers there, I suddenly remember that I'm shirtless and only wearing my boxers.

"Shit." I snatch up my jeans and hurry back into them. "Sorry, I wasn't thinking." As I yank my shirt back over my head and collect myself, I notice she's eyeing the sand shyly. The moon's light on her face reveals the redness of her cheeks.

"Um, we should go back and check on Claudia," she says, turning.

"Yeah." I grab my sneakers and fall in step beside her. "Oh, are we still on for that tour Sunday?"

I'm looking forward to spending more time with her.

My excitement grows with her nod. "Sure, Claudia's coming with us."

No! What the hell!

"Oh," I mutter, hiding my distress. "That's cool."

We keep walking in silence until I ask, "How long have you and Nate been together?"

The look on her face turns distant, like my bringing him up makes her consider something. "Um, since April."

"Wow, barely before finishing high school, huh?" If I had gone to the same school as Reign, I never would've waited that long to ask her out.

She parts her lips to say more, but a raspy voice shouts her name from the steps at the side of the house.

Nate. That's just great.

He stomps toward us, almost tripping over his own feet. He's buzzed.

"Been looking for you, babe." He pulls her to his side and glances from Reign to me. "What's going on?"

I hate the harshness in his tone. "Hey—"

"Nothing," Reign intervenes. "I went for a walk, and Micah was out here, too. We were heading back."

He squints while searching my face. "Aren't you that new waiter at Cap... ahem," He breaks to compose himself. "*Captain's Choice*?" Glancing around the beach, he flicks back to me, saying with a scowl, "Dude, why are you even at this party? You don't know any of us."

There's that damn attitude again.

"I came with Claudia," I reply flatly. "And I know Reign—I mean," I start to retract my statement as his eyebrows shoot up. "She said it would be cool if I came."

Nate snorts. "Whatever." He directs his attention to Reign. "Let's go back to the party, babe. You're sleeping over. Ryan's cool with it."

My throat tightens.

It irks me to hear him say that to her. I know he's her boyfriend, yet every fiber of me is begging her to tell him no.

Reign peers over at me for a beat and looks down at the sand, uncomfortable.

"I can't," she says, shutting him down. "I have to make sure Claudia gets home okay."

Oh shit! I almost break out into a happy dance.

His face stiffens, and he flashes me a look of embarrassment.

"Okay," he says in a low tone. "Let's find her and get you girls home then."

He places his arm around her and leads her toward the house. I follow behind, making sure to keep my distance.

Reaching the deck, I notice most of the kids from earlier have left. I spot Claudia near the pool, drinking and dancing to the soundless music in her head because the DJ has already packed up his equipment and is preparing to take off.

Reign walks over and touches her elbow. "Claudia, give me your keys. I'll drive."

She laughs and throws her arms around Reign, slurring, "Surrre, Reigneee. Whatever…" *Burp.* "… you say."

I move forward to help. Nate beats me to it, taking Claudia from Reign to carry her down the steps to her jeep. Reign picks up her bag and rifles for the keys before heading out. I pace behind her and sidetrack to the gate to walk home.

As Nate settles Claudia in the back and shuts the door, Reign hops in behind the wheel, starting the engine. He moves to her door, leaning in the window to kiss her cheek. "Drive safe, babe, and text me when you get home. I'll hang out here for the night."

She nods and looks out the windshield. Our eyes meet. *Why am I still standing here?*

I turn to leave.

"Micah," Reign calls out to me, adding when I look back, "Get in. I'll drive you home."

Delight swells in my chest, settling as I glimpse Nate's screwed-up face.

"Don't you have a car?" he grits.

"He doesn't," Reign tells him. "That's why I'm offering him a ride. We invited him, so I want to take him home."

He looks at her with palpable irritation. She keeps her eyes on me, though, waiting for me to enter the jeep.

Nate stares me down as I move away from the gate and approach the jeep, settling in the passenger seat.

Watching him fume feels good. He seems to be the jealous type, and he should be. I might steal his girlfriend after all.

Acting territorial again, Nate sticks his head in the window and kisses her softly. "Bye, babe. See you on Sunday?" His eyes have a sneaky spark as if he's reminding her of their plans.

"See you," Reign says lowly before driving out the gates.

TWELVE

Reign

CLAUDIA KEEPS ALTERNATING between moaning and giggling to herself on the backseat. None of what she's saying makes sense. It's hard for us not to laugh.

I like Micah's deep, raspy, and sexy laugh.

Is it wrong for me to notice?

"So, where are you taking me on Sunday?" he asks, starting a conversation to drown out Claudia's mumbling.

"Uh, we can check out some historical sites and such," I reply.

"Sounds boring. Remember, I'm looking for excitement."

"It'll be exciting," I counter, looking over at him briefly before I return my eyes to the road.

"Nah, I don't think you're fun. You didn't want to get in the water tonight when I tried to be spontaneous."

Micah's only kidding, but he has no idea how afraid I am. I'd love to have the courage to jump in the ocean, but every time I go near the edge, I see Mary's face. She's waiting for me.

"Hey," he breaks me out of my thoughts with a soft chuckle. "I was joking. Don't think so hard. You might have a breakdown."

"I'm not," I force a laugh.

There's an unsettling silence between us before Micah goes to say something again, only Claudia cackles loudly. We both yelp in surprise.

Peering back to check on her, he straightens and whistles, "Wow, she's had quite a few."

I flip on my right indicator as we approach his street. "She's usually not like this. It only happens once in a while." I should make Claudia look good to Micah since she wants to go out with him. However, I feel a strange prick when I think about them dating, as if I don't want it to happen.

"Whatever the case," he says, "it's good she has a friend that looks out for her."

"Thanks. I try."

I glance over to smile at him and then look straight ahead as I approach his house. "Well, here you are."

Micah unbuckles his seatbelt but doesn't hop out immediately, as if he has something on his mind. He parts his lips, yet nothing comes out.

"Is there... something you want to say?" I press, curious.

Finally, he meets my gaze. "See you at work."

"Oh, yeah, see you."

"One... more... c'mon..." Claudia rambles, her words punctuated by burps. Micah looks over at her again and shakes his head. "She's gonna have a wicked headache tomorrow."

"Indeed, she will."

He climbs out of the jeep and shuts the door, waving at me as he makes his way to the house and steps inside. I drive off right after.

THIRTEEN

Micah

BEFORE THE SUN fully brightens the place, I run and end up at the cliff walk behind the mansions overlooking the ocean. There aren't that many people because it's so early. I wasn't expecting to see Reign.

Slowing down, I take in her physique as she bends over to stretch her back and hamstrings. Her workout tights show off her round butt. I lick my lips and fantasize about cupping those cheeks in my hands, feeling their firmness.

I jog up to her as she stretches from side to side. "Morning."

"Morning," she replies, turning with her face scrunched up in curiosity. "I didn't know you knew about this place."

I shrug. "Not until today. I usually push myself to the limit, so I figured I'd go the extra mile. Hence, how I ended up here."

"Cool." She bobs slowly, an impressed smile playing on her lips. "Well, I'm just getting started. Not too tired to run to the end of the cliff walk with me?"

"Sure." *As if I'd refuse.*

We jog the rest of the way without saying a word. I do my best to squash my gasps and the fact that I'm almost out of breath. It's hard when I'm having a difficult time keeping my eyes off her body, especially the way her butt bounces with every trek.

It's like she's in slow motion as I watch her chest rise and fall. And the sexy way her lips part to release steady breaths. I wish we could run together every morning.

Reign looks over at me for a second and smiles. "You seem to be keeping up all right after covering so much already."

If only she knew.

The killer thing about it is I have to run the same frigging distance back. Great! Then again, I guess it's worth it—I get to spend a little time with Reign.

We finally reach the end, and I hunch over, unable to contain my exhaustion any longer.

"Oh gosh." Reign opens the fanny pack around her waist and takes out a water bottle. "Here, drink this."

I accept it quickly, straighten up, and gulp down the water. It quenches my thirst, but I don't drain the bottle, in case it's her only one.

Putting the cap on, I hand it back to her. She takes a sip and then gives it back to me. I delay taking the bottle. Wasn't that an indirect kiss? And aren't I going to taste her lips now?

My heart thumps as she says, "Drink some more."

"You sure?" I confirm, stifling my childish excitement as I take the bottle from her.

She nods. I waste no time finishing what's left. I taste her lips; it's sugary sweet, like candy chapstick. I love it.

As my breathing stabilizes, Reign approaches the fence and peers at the sea. The sun's starting to rise. I control my raging hormones and step up to her side, never taking my eyes off her as she admires the sky.

How can one person appear so divine whenever the sunlight catches her face? She leaves me breathless.

"Want to start back now?" she asks, facing me. I don't drop my eyes from her, even though she knows I must have been staring.

"You're really beautiful," I say, looking at her again.

Smiling shyly, she glances at the ground and wipes her forehead with the back of her hand. As if dismissing my compliment, Reign gestures over my shoulder. "Let's head back."

She steps past me. I pace behind, feeling like I shouldn't have said anything. But what's wrong with telling her she's beautiful, even if I'm not her boyfriend? Is that a crime?

Reign doesn't utter a word until we reach our starting point. She motions me toward the parking area.

"I'll drive you back," she offers as we approach her car.

"Thanks," I say, happy to get off my feet and ecstatic to stay with her longer despite her weird reaction to my compliment.

Backing out of the parking lot, she pulls onto the main road and takes off for my house. I keep my mouth shut. No more compliments, for now.

FOURTEEN

Reign

I READ ONCE that something's wrong if you look at another guy longer than you stare at your boyfriend. And while I know this, I can't stop looking at Micah. His compliment from earlier keeps playing over and over in my head. The genuine way he said it and how his eyes pierced me like steel made me feel desired in a way I've never been before.

"Close your mouth," Aislin whispers at my back.

I whip around and eye her innocently. "Excuse me?"

"You were so drooling over Micah," she teases. "You've been staring at him since he walked in the door."

That's true. I can only think about his muscular legs in those running shorts and the stimulating way sweat dripped down his face. He looked like one of those toned guys from a workout commercial.

"Hello, Reign?" She snaps her fingers before my eyes. "Focus here."

I roll my eyes and walk to the deck, gripping the railing.

Aislin comes up beside me. "If it makes a difference, I've noticed him staring at you, too."

"Stop it," I tell her.

"Come on. He's cute. No harm in checking him out."

"You sound like Claudia."

She bumps my arm lightly and looks at the water. I use the opportunity to ask about her issue with Nate. "Why have you been acting annoyed about my boyfriend?"

Aislin shrugs and then meets my gaze. "Let's just say, if you're looking at another guy like that, he's not doing something right."

She walks off without saying anything else. I can't help but ponder her words. Maybe because Nate keeps initiating sex with me in more ways than just asking is pushing me away. If that's the case, my attraction to Micah is only a phase.

Nothing more.

"Why are you always contemplating so hard?"

My body shudders at his husky voice. I tighten my grip on the railing and keep staring ahead while my heart hammers behind my ribcage.

Micah hoists up the umbrella on the table nearby and walks over, looking out at the harbor. This time, I allow myself to consume his earthy scent. It plays with my nerves, stirring up an intense feeling in my chest.

Frick! This phase needs to hurry up and pass.

I turn my head just as he glances at me. When our eyes lock, heat trickles across my skin. Uncontrollably, I move closer as if trying to graze his hand like that night.

What the hell am I doing? I have a boyfriend.

Micah places his hands on the railing as his eyes shift to my lips. His Adam's apple bobs as he slowly lowers his head, coming closer than the appropriate distance between us.

But I can't move.

I really can't.

He inches closer to my mouth. I gasp, parting my lips to inhale him. He's almost there when a burst of laughter interrupts the moment.

I spin away to see Aislin leading a group onto the deck. Collecting myself, I hurry back inside the restaurant.

Micah almost kissed me. I can't believe I nearly let him. We have to maintain the distance between us. I can't allow him to make me question my feelings for Nate like that.

For the rest of the day, I avoid Micah. I don't look his way. I don't speak to him. I even avoid going out on the deck—my thinking spot. Nothing to make me repeat our earlier mistake.

That's what it was—a mistake.

As evening creeps in, I stand by my car and wait for him to leave the restaurant. When he does, I stroll up to him. "I have something to say to you."

He nods. "Okay."

"Micah, you seem like a cool guy, and I'd like us to be friends, so..." I take control of the rising heat inside before it overpowers me. Looking into his eyes messes with my senses. "Um..."

"I get it," he says with a grin. "You think I'm feeling you and don't want me to ruin your relationship."

"I... guess."

He chuckles softly. "Seriously, Reign, you need to relax. I'm not trying to mess up what you have with Nate. I want to be friends, too. Only that."

A part of me is relieved, and a part of me is upset. I'm not even sure which part I'm leaning more toward, and I can't help but notice the expression on his face, which doesn't seem like he means what he said.

"Good," I say. "I just wanted to make things clear."

"There's nothing to clarify. We're friends. It's not like I want you to give me a ride home where I'll lure you into my apartment, seduce you into my bed, and spend the night making love to you."

"Uh," I gasp and back up a few steps.

A broad grin spreads across his face, and he steps forward. "Again, kidding."

I'm not appalled by his audacious remark, only surprised at myself for considering it when I've never even slept with my boyfriend.

He peers over my shoulder and says, "I have to catch the trolley. I don't want a ride with you looking at me like that."

"What do you mean? How am I looking at you?" I blurt out.

"Like you're afraid of what I'll do to you."

His eyes penetrate mine, searching for the truth. I shake my head and tilt my chin up bravely. "I'm not afraid. We're just friends."

"Cool. Still, I'd rather catch the trolley."

He walks past me. I let him go. He's right. I don't think I can drive him home tonight, not with these thoughts of wanting him to touch and kiss me running wild through my head.

"Oh," he says in an afterthought and spins around. "What?"

"Are we still on for my tour in the morning?"

I nod.

He flashes that sexy smile that pricks my tummy before hurrying to the trolley.

Geez. This guy is turning me into a very bad girl.

FIFTEEN

Micah

IT'S ALMOST seven-thirty now. I wonder if we'll have enough time to hang out before work at ten. I pace around the apartment until I hear a knock at the door. My stomach starts to do that thing again because I expect it to be Reign.

"Hi!" Claudia waves when I open the door.

Her smile dwindles as she observes my reaction. It's too hard to hide my disappointment.

"Hey," I say, trying to sound nice.

She peeks inside. "Mind if I come in?"

"Why?" I ask, "Aren't we taking off now?"

"Geez, Micah. I want to see your spot. Is that so bad?" There's a mischievous grin stretching her bright red lips. I know I shouldn't, but I figure why not—get it over with so we can leave.

I invite her in. Claudia sashays by me in her blue, thigh-high cami dress with a cut-out back and wedge sandals. Her legs are pretty toned. I can't help looking at them as she peers around.

Glancing back at me, she smiles. "It's open. I like it."

"Cool. Ready to go?"

"What's the rush?" She walks back to me by the door.

I shrug. "Reign and I have to be at work soon, so it's better to get going."

She edges closer and places her hand on my neck, caressing it. "Micah, I've been thinking about you. A lot."

Claudia eyes my chest as she speaks. Then she bites down on her bottom lip and rests both hands on my stomach, feeling my abs.

"God, you're hot," she squeals.

"Okay, stop it." I remove her hands from my body and back up into the doorway. "Let's go."

Her smile fades. "Go? But I just got here." She slants and looks over at my bed, nodding toward it as she says playfully, "Let's have some fun before the tour."

She's either bold or desperate, none too far from the other. It only means that she believes in no strings attached like me. But I'm not so sure I'm looking for flings anymore. Even though she's throwing herself at me, I'm not interested.

I only want Reign.

"Claudia, I... um... I think you should go. We'll do the tour another time." I motion for her to leave.

Wrinkling her thin brows, she sweeps her long red hair off her shoulders and scoffs as she struts past me into the hallway. She lingers there, surprised a guy rejected her. "Is there something wrong? I thought you weren't looking for commitment."

I don't want to hurt her feelings, but I have to clarify so she no longer has any hope of us hooking up. "Listen, you're a beautiful girl; any guy would be lucky to have you. I'm just not interested in being anything other than your friend without benefits."

Shifting her weight from one leg to the other, she chews at the inside of her mouth. "Is there someone else you're interested in hooking up with?"

"No," I quickly deny. "I'm not looking to hook up with anyone."

Claudia eyes me for a moment, not uttering a word. The air grows tense. I'm about to make up an excuse about having something to do when she seems to forget her attempts at seducing me. "I'm sorry about that. Let's pretend it never happened and go hang out. Reign and I would love to help you feel welcomed here."

I pause a moment to consider it and then decide why not. I do want to go, after all.

"Okay," I say. "Gimme a sec." I grab my keys and cell phone, walk out the door, and head downstairs behind Claudia. She's all smiles again.

And so am I.

The tour is more fun than expected. Newport truly is a cool place. Its historic features and the ocean easily sweep up a newbie like me. Everywhere I go, I see water. The lifestyle is relaxing. I haven't thought about what happened in Haxtun or seen my gram's face again since that day I had a momentary relapse at the restaurant.

We can't check out much, so we decide to continue another day and drive to a café for breakfast. It's all fun and cool conversation until Reign's cell phone buzzes.

She looks at the screen, and her expression switches to uncertainty. I wonder what's troubling her.

Claudia's going on about a bonfire on the beach later tonight, but I remain focused on Reign, hoping she'll glance my way and I'll somehow make her smile again. Gosh, I like her smile. She looks nice with her hair let down, and her floral dress is cute. I wish it were windy so I could see those legs.

"Hey," Claudia says, grabbing our attention. "You two listening, or am I talking to myself?"

"Yeah," Reign and I answer at the same time. Finally, she meets my gaze. My heart thuds as she smiles halfway.

"So, anyway," Claudia continues, "Micah, are you coming to the bonfire?"

"I don't know. I feel like a bother, letting you girls drive me around."

"It's no problem," Reign says fast. "I don't mind." She drops her eyes to her spoonful of clam chowder.

I replay what she just said, looking down at my plate to try and hide the grin that's fighting to spread across my face. When I recover and look up again, I glimpse Claudia. She's studying us carefully.

"So," she chimes in, "Micah, where in Colorado are you from?"

Oh no. I've been doing great, not thinking about my hometown or what I left behind. "Haxtun."

She thinks for a moment and then frowns. "Never heard of it. What's fun there?"

I lean back in the chair, answering dryly, "Nothing. Depends on what's fun to you."

Sipping her coffee, Claudia continues questioning me. "If you were back in Haxtun now, what would you do on the weekend?" She's oblivious or uncaring that my body language screams, 'I don't want to talk about it.'

I glance at Reign. She has her eyes narrowed, curious about me, too.

"Probably wasted and being a complete jerk to everyone," I reply.

Claudia scoffs.

"I don't believe that," Reign says. I look at her. "I find it hard to see you that way."

Folding my arms, I smirk and say sarcastically, "Well, need I remind you that you don't know me?"

"So far, you seem like a pretty level-headed guy. You didn't have one beer at Ryan's party and didn't seem tempted to wild out like everyone else."

I loosen my arms and rest my elbows on the table to get closer to her. "What if it's a show? What if this nice guy thing is all an act?"

She tilts her head to one side and says confidently, "The guy I saw walking on the beach Friday night who tried to get me to go swimming was not putting on a show."

"Oh, yeah?" I snort.

Reign bobs her head. "I'm usually a good judge of character. I can tell you're genuinely a nice guy."

"Good judge of character, huh?" I tease. "Then what about Nate?" Oops, didn't mean to let that slip. Hmm... maybe I did.

Astonished, she blinks profusely and eases back in her seat. "What about him?"

"Um, hello?" Claudia pipes in, waving her hand. "I'm still here."

I seem to have caused tension between me and Reign. She turns away from me and motions to the waitress for the bill. "We should get going. The restaurant opens in thirty minutes," she mutters, not looking at me.

"Okay, yeah." Claudia pulls her clutch from her lap and places it on the table, rifling through her wallet.

I stop her. "Don't. I'll take care of it."

Reign stares at me again. "We took you out. There's no way we can ask you to pay for breakfast. Let's split it three ways."

Waving her off, I reach into my pocket and take out my wallet. "I wouldn't be a gentleman then."

Claudia swoons. "Aw, that's so sweet of you."

I look at Reign as I leave a couple of bills and the tip on the table.

She smiles while squinting at me. "See? A nice guy."

SIXTEEN

Reign

I DON'T UNDERSTAND NATE. He's been texting me flirty things.

Anticipation babe.

Can't think of anything else.

R u ready?

Can't wait to be inside U.

I haven't replied to any. Anxiety has been chewing at my insides all day. I tell myself to get it over with, but shortly before I leave work, he texts me that he won't be able to pick me up and that I should meet him at the bonfire.

Since I left my car at home, I drive there with Claudia and Micah, who she convinced to come out with us. Being around Micah is nice. When I'm with him, I feel *relaxed*. And I feel so safe.

I haven't felt that way since Mary died.

Still, I'm convinced that my attraction to him—based on his hotness—is only temporary. Whatever is happening will disappear once I know him better as a friend. The beginning of the end starts tonight when I sleep with Nate.

Arriving at the beach, I spot Nate with Ryan and other guys from our graduating class. He breaks away from them when he finally glimpses me. It's hard to let him stick his alcohol-laced tongue inside my mouth. I let him kiss my lips instead, no matter how he's trying to go deeper. In times like this, I don't want to kiss him back. It's not romantic.

At the end of the kiss, he tows me into his arms, a scowl forming as he regards Micah.

"You again?" he sneers.

Claudia snakes her arm around Micah's and says, "Yes, him again. Got a problem?"

Micah doesn't say anything. He only looks at Nate hard, his sea blue eyes darkened by the night, annoyance morphing his face.

Nate lifts his beer to his lips and scoffs before having a drink. "Anyway." He turns me to face him, stroking my cheek. "Sorry you had to come here, babe. I know it's not your scene, but my parents hadn't left yet for their little out-of-town thing."

Claudia titters knowingly. I sneak a glance at Micah. He's looking out at the ocean, trying to hide his frustration.

But why is he upset?

Throwing his arm around me, Nate draws me up the beach. I peer back at my best friend. I don't know why. Maybe for confirmation that I'm doing the right thing?

She shrugs and pulls Micah toward the fire, introducing him to everyone.

I refocus on Nate and let him haul me to his car. My heart starts to pound as we slip inside, and he immediately takes off for his house.

When we arrive and enter the front door, he picks me up in his arms and carries me down the hall to his bedroom.

My expectations are probably too high, but he said he'd make tonight special. He promised.

As he pushes the door open and settles me back on my feet, I see clothes all over the floor, his bed messy, and a poster of Beyoncé's Sports Illustrated cover hanging above it.

Wow.

Maybe I'm putting too much into this, but the least he could do is play romantic music if rose petals and candles aren't his style.

My heart feels like it's about to burst through my ribcage when he places his hand on the small of my back, guiding me over to his bed. Nate pushes a towel and shirt out of the way, and then he gently lowers me down, kissing me again.

He brings his hands to my arms, massaging them. Then he climbs over me. I squeeze my eyes shut when he moves his mouth from my lips and kisses my neck.

Trailing his hands down, he pulls up my dress and caresses my legs. I shiver at his touch as his fingertips travel a path up my thighs to trace the edge of my underwear.

Surprisingly, Micah's smile flashes across my mind. I begin envisioning *him* touching me this way instead. I can't help the heatwave that it sends through my body.

I quickly open my eyes and try to erase the image of another guy.

Nate eases up. Hauling his shirt over his head, he looks down at me, groans, and licks his lips. He pulls my dress up further and touches my stomach.

"Want to take it off?" he asks in a flirty tone I haven't heard him use before.

I'm still so nervous, and it's not the good kind. It's not the one where desire fills up your body so much you can't wait to go further. It's the kind of nervousness where you can't shake the feeling that what's about to happen feels too damn wrong. And why does he have the stupid poster hanging over his bed? I love Beyoncé too, but not above my boyfriend. She's the last thing he sees at night before he sleeps and the first in the morning when he wakes up.

Gawd! Why is losing my virginity to my boyfriend tripping me out so much? And why do I keep seeing Micah's eyes?

"Reign?" Nate draws me out of my thoughts. I wince as he touches my hips and tugs at my underwear.

"No, please stop," I whisper, pushing against the headboard.

He stops and looks at my face, confused. "What? What do you mean?"

I slide out from under him, stepping away from the bed as I fix my dress and say almost breathlessly, "I don't want to do this."

Nate laughs short and stares at me like I've gone insane. He gets off the bed, stepping closer. "You don't want to do this?" he repeats. "You're changing your mind after getting me so riled up?"

I dislike how he's talking, so I back away to put distance between us. "I'm sorry, but I'm not ready."

"You told me only three days ago that you were."

"I know, but... you were getting mad and..."

"And what?" he presses.

I look him straight in the eye as I say, "You were pressuring me."

His jaw stiffens. He exhales deeply and eyes the floor. Seconds later, he calms down and edges closer to me, draping his arms around my body. "I'm sorry. I didn't mean to do that. You know I'd never force you to do anything, right?"

I lift my hands to his back, hugging him in return. "I don't understand why we can't wait a while," I mutter at his neck.

Tightening his grasp, Nate kisses me on the side of my head and says softly, "We can wait as long as you want."

Relief floods me. How can I stay mad at this guy, much less not fall for him? He's a good guy, so why's it hard to love him?

Easing me out of his embrace, Nate plants another kiss on my mouth. This time, I part my lips, regardless of the taste of liquor on his tongue.

Then we walk out of his bedroom, hand in hand, and he drives me home.

As he pulls up at my house, I reach over the middle console and kiss him on the cheek before getting out of the car. He takes off when I open the front door and walk inside.

While lying in bed trying to fall asleep, I replay what happened and how Nate got over my reaction. And oddly, my mind drifts to Micah again. I wonder what he's doing. If he had a good time at the bonfire and if he and Claudia made any progress. A selfish part of me wishes they didn't.

SEVENTEEN

Micah

I WENT OUT for a run early Monday morning, but sadly, I didn't see Reign on the cliff walk. So, at work, I spend my time stealing glances at her. Reign, on the other hand, is being evasive.

It was obvious Nate wanted them to leave the bonfire last night so that he could sleep with her. That burned me. I took off shortly after they left. As cool as Claudia was, now that she's toning down her flirtation, I couldn't hang out somewhere that I only went to in the first place because of Reign.

Still, I can tell something isn't right. Usually, girls look happy the day after sex if they enjoy it. So if Reign did, there'd be a glow to her. She'd be happy-go-lucky.

She hasn't smiled one bit.

It slows down by afternoon, so she strolls out back to take a break. I sneak out behind her, wanting to know what's wrong and if that boyfriend of hers did something.

"Hey," I say, moseying over to stand beside her with my back against the wall. "You okay? You seem kind of off."

She looks at me amazed. "It's only been a week since you started working here. How do you know when I'll be off?"

I stare at her, searching those gorgeous hazel eyes. Then I ask her in a deeper tone than my natural voice, "Would you think I'm weird if I say I've memorized every expression?"

She's unable to stifle back her smile. I feel elated knowing I'm responsible for it. "Um, yeah, that's kind of weird," she manages to say.

I shrug. "I don't mind being weird. But tell me, you don't feel even the slightest bit impressed by the fact that I've noticed things about you? I mean, what girl doesn't like that?"

Reign looks up at my face, observing my features intensely. No words pass between us, only the sound of the ocean and sailboats in the distance.

"Are you and Claudia together now?" she asks with a speck of disappointment.

"Why? Are you jealous?" I tease.

She perks up, twisting her mouth. "Pfft... I'm not. I could care less."

"Is that so?"

"Yeah." She's trying hard to appear unfazed. I can tell it's a front.

I take the chance to inch closer to her, wanting to have contact. Whether it's to touch her arm, stroke her cheek, or even brush my lips against hers. I want to graze her like that night when we hung out alone by the pier. The problem is, will she let me?

My attempt at the railing on Saturday was a disappointment. Even though she's pushing us to be friends, I can tell she's having trouble hiding her attraction to me. She wanted that kiss.

I draw close enough that we are toe to toe. Light flickers in her gorgeous eyes and her chest rises and falls deeply. I'm making her nervous.

Taking an even bigger risk, I drop my hands from my pockets and lift one to run across her cheek. I move slowly, holding her gaze like I've placed her under a spell. She doesn't back away, so I consider it a sign that she'll let me get closer.

I'm almost there when the backdoor pushes open. Aislin peeps out. "What are you two doing? I have a room full of vacationers in here."

Reign collects herself and hurries past me. I delay to silently fume over the interruption, shake it off, and go back to work.

"Micah," Mrs. Aldridge calls out to me before I can leave for the day. The restaurant's closing, and I'm hoping to convince Reign to hang out with me since Claudia isn't here to bug me about another party or something. But it looks like her mom has other plans for me.

I look over, and she gestures for me to accompany her to the office. That's when I remember the background check.

Shit! Shit! Shit!

I'm pretty much screwed. She's going to fire me. That means I'll have no way of being around Reign. I don't know if we'll even be friends when her mom tells her I've been in juvie.

"Have a seat, Micah," she says as we enter the office.

I sit down and mentally prepare myself for her questions. "What's up?" I ask, trying to seem casual.

Sitting down, Mrs. Aldridge clasps her hands on the desk and peers at me as the Judge did before giving me her sentence.

"Micah." My body tenses when she says my name. "I'm sure you know what this is about?"

I slump my shoulders, accepting defeat. I'm about to be fired for sure. "I'm sorry I lied about my name. It was only to get the job."

She sighs deeply and collapses back in the chair. "The courts sealed your records, *Mitchel Stephens,* so I have no idea why you were in a juvenile detention center for eight months."

I look down at my hands. My palms are starting to sweat. Knots twist in my stomach. And the horrible memory of what happened begins to play in my head.

"I'm not judging you, Micah. I've worked at a center for troubled teens, so I know there aren't all bad apples in the bunch."

I wrench myself out of it to glance up at her.

She dips her head. "I worked in Providence years before I married and moved to Newport. I guess that's how I can tell you're a good kid. I'm curious how you landed yourself in that kind of trouble."

Easing forward, she goes through the papers on top of her desk. "I found a newspaper article from Haxtun. It says here that many were baffled by what happened. You were always helpful to your grandmother, played on your high school soccer team, had good grades—"

"Please don't go through that," I stop her.

She looks up at me, eyes narrowed. I can see fine wrinkles as she creases her forehead. Now that I'm looking at her closely, Reign doesn't resemble Mrs. Aldridge that much.

"Micah, I'm not asking you to tell me what happened. But I do hope that this traveling you're doing isn't a result of you trying to escape your past."

That's exactly what I'm doing. Why is she turning into my shrink now?

"I'm not," I lie. "I always wanted to travel."

Her face relaxes, and she gives me a tight-lipped smile. Nodding, she sticks the papers back inside a folder and slips them into one of her drawers.

"Well, I won't keep you any longer," she says, standing up.

I rise as well, amazed that she's not firing me. "Thank you for not letting me go," I tell her, grateful.

Mrs. Aldridge waves me off. "I guess I'm too much of a softy. And you're a good worker. This place needs you until I decide—" She doesn't finish.

And I don't ask, only smile before turning to walk out of her office. Mrs. Aldridge is a nice lady. That much Reign has taken from her. I wonder what Mr. Aldridge is like.

When I rush outside and look down the street, the trolley has already left. It's a good walk from the restaurant to my house, but I don't have a choice. I have to tread home tonight.

I walk for a little before headlights shine on me. She pulls over and nods for me to get in. "I saw the trolley take off, and I knew you weren't on it, so I waited around to give you a ride."

"Thanks," I say, climbing into the car. I hope my grin isn't too much and isn't freaking her out.

Reign drives off. I notice she doesn't turn left toward my street.

"This is exciting," I tease. "You're kidnapping me."

She giggles. "Gosh, you're so silly. I thought you'd like to watch a live acoustic performance, so I'm taking you to Pure Bistro." *You can take me anywhere, baby.*

"Pure Bistro?" I repeat, enthusiastic. "That's an interesting name. Does it only accommodate untainted people? Cause if that's the case, I probably shouldn't go. I might tarnish the place. Burst into flames, so to speak."

Reign laughs. "Don't worry. I'm sure they'll make an exception for you."

I smirk. "Based on what?"

"Based on the fact that you're charming," she says, in a way that seems like she doesn't realize she said it. "I mean... you're a cool guy. I'm sure they'll see that, too."

I laugh. "Admit it. You think I'm hot."

"What? No... I," she fumbles. "I didn't say that."

"It's okay. I think you're hot, too."

Reign falls quiet. Light from passing traffic blares on her face, and I can see red cheeks. She tightens her grip on the wheel and slightly shifts in her seat. Oh yeah, I'm getting under her skin.

EIGHTEEN

Reign

I HAVEN'T been to the Pure Bistro since my eighteenth birthday last July, so I'm excited to go there tonight. A local artist I follow, Allysen Callery, is performing. She's been touring for a while and can finally stop in Newport. Several nights ago, I asked Nate to accompany me to her first performance, but he said her music wasn't his cup of tea. And, of course, Claudia likes to dance.

"This is Pure?" asks Micah, sounding taken aback. He strolls inside the bistro next to me. As we approach the hostess, he peers around and checks everything out. "It's cool."

"There's always good music. It's probably not what you listen to, but it's a vibe."

"It does sound nice," he says, glancing at me with a delightful grin. I'm only now seeing he has a dimple at the right corner of his mouth. Gosh, it's sexy.

He notices me staring. I quickly look away to hide my flushed cheeks and pick at the loops of my jeans.

The hostess leaves us to find a table.

Allysen is already singing, her voice like a calm rainfall soothing to the soul. I wonder if this bores Micah like Nate. I wonder if he's only pretending to be into it because he feels obligated since I'm driving him home.

Even though I want to listen to the artist, I feel happier he's here with me. I don't even know why.

All I know is I think of nothing else when he's around—not about my inner guilt about Mary's death, much less about Nate. My mind is completely free right now.

And I like it.

The hostess returns and leads us to a table in the back. Micah takes in the folk singer, strumming effortlessly on her guitar. She engulfs the room in this exhilarating acoustic atmosphere.

"Who is she?" he asks.

"Allysen Callery," I reply, gushing. "She's one of my favorites."

He looks at me with a knowing flare in his eyes. "I can see why." His words send a wintry sensation down my back.

Sitting at the table, I thank the hostess before asking Micah, "What do you mean?"

He doesn't say anything, only stares at me and smiles. Feeling uneasy, I divert my attention to Allysen to settle the butterflies flying wildly in my stomach.

My gosh. He stirs me up so much. It's wrong. I shouldn't even be out with him if I feel this way. But I can't help myself. I'm different when I'm with Micah; it seems almost like I'm a prisoner to my attraction.

A waitress fills our glasses with water, and we order non-alcoholic drinks.

"What kind of music do you listen to?" I ask him when she walks away.

Micah relaxes back in the chair, telling me, "Mostly indie rock. I don't listen to anything mainstream."

"Yeah, me neither."

Allysen finishes *I Had a Lover I Thought Was My Own* and transitions into *Spare Parts* amid the applause.

Micah cuts from my gaze and looks at her, listening to the words. Palpable mystery overshadows his face like the song has transported him into a memory he can't share. My fascination grows as his eyes lower to the glass of water on the table. It is one of my favorites. The song arouses me even more, seeing how it impacts him.

Micah stays adrift for a few more seconds until the waitress returns with our drinks. As he steers his eyes back to me, his lips curl into a half-smile.

I want to ask what's on his mind, but that's too personal. We still have to get to know each other better. I mean, as friends. *Friends.* I must embed that in my head.

"So, any college plans? What do you want to do?" I ask as the song comes to an end.

Setting his drink on the table, he pauses for a beat before answering. "I'm not sure college is for me. Education is great, but there are other things I'd like to do right now."

"Like what?" I prod.

He stares at my lips, and instead of answering, he asks, "Do you love him?"

My chest tightens. Suddenly thirsty, I grab my drink and chug half of my mocktail—a fruity elderberry shrub. It does nothing for me.

"Why'd you ask that?" I mutter afterward, trying to act cool.

"It's a simple question," he smirks. "You either love your boyfriend or you don't."

My stomach flutters. I wish Allysen would start singing another song. "I don't understand why you'd ask that suddenly."

"I don't think you do," he says, so sure as he studies my face.

My cheeks heat up under his gaze. I'm back in high school, crushing on someone. That strange feeling is back in my gut.

Micah's right. I don't know how he figured it out, though. He met me days ago and already knows me.

I *don't* love Nate. I like him. That's why it's so hard to sleep with him. There's a difference between those two words. I thought by now that *like* would transition into *love*—into something deeper—but it hasn't.

Will it ever?

Ugh! Why am I second-guessing my relationship because of this guy? *Damn you, Micah.* And why's he looking at me like that? Like he wants to reach across the table and kiss me.

"Uh, I have to go the restroom." I stand up.

He shrugs and sips his drink as I walk away.

Going into the restroom, I look in the mirror before splashing water on my flushed face. This was a bad idea.

Coming here with Micah has worsened my attraction. If anything, it's increased. I can't get his eyes off my mind. They keep haunting me.

Drying my face with a napkin, I linger to settle my thoughts and open the door, gasping when I see Micah waiting nearby. He walks down the passage to the back door, gesturing for me to follow him.

I do.

Micah pushes the door open and steps into the warm night. Two girls are sharing the same cigarette. They check us out, discard it, and head back inside as if to give us privacy.

"What's up?" I ask, nervously sauntering over to him as he stares at the starry sky. The lights from the town nearby flicker in the distance. I can hear the ocean. If this was a romantic date, we could walk down to the beach and stroll along the shore.

It's not.

"Ever since that day in the park, I can't get you off my mind," he reveals with his back turned to me.

I search my head, having no idea what he's talking about. "You saw me in a park? When?"

Micah turns to face me, determination in his eyes. He edges closer. Reflexively, I take a step back. He advances until I'm against the building's brick wall. He places his hands on either side of my head, staring at me intensely. I slope my head as if anticipating what he'll do next.

"My first day in Newport," he whispers. "The weekend before I started working for your mom, I saw you in that park by the harbor. You wore a blue dress, and you'd let your hair down like now." Goosebumps break out across my skin as he wraps a finger around a strand. "And I felt mesmerized."

Oh! So that's where I've seen him before. "That was you..." I trail, thinking back to the day. I only saw him briefly as I ran off to meet Claudia, but I remember now.

He caresses my cheek. I shiver, knowing what he wants to do and how much I secretly want it to happen. I've wanted it for days.

I can see it in his eyes, and I feel so imprisoned by desire that I have no room left in my brain to consider the consequences.

"You're so beautiful," he rasps, lowering his head. His minty breath bathes my cheeks, igniting a fire between my legs.

Micah drops both hands only to grip my waist. His eyes sweep over me. Without hesitation, he presses his body against mine, his lips scant inches away from my mouth. The temperature has grown impeccably hot. I can feel the bulge in his jeans against my thigh.

"Um... Micah, maybe we shouldn't..." I say breathlessly, engulfed in the heat.

He gently presses one finger to my lips and whispers, "Shh. Just let it happen."

His gaze captivates me as he moves his finger from my lips and comes in for a kiss, only to pull away abruptly as the door pushes open and a few people step outside to smoke.

They smile at us knowingly. Having my senses snap back to me, I step around Micah and scurry back inside.

He emerges as Allysen wraps her segment with my favorite song, *See the Sea*. It's funny how the lyrics sound different now that I'm sitting across from a guy I almost kissed.

Oh, what am I going to do?

We don't say anything. We only slip out of the bistro right after Allysen finishes.

I drive him home, which I probably should have done to begin with, and avoid the uneasiness.

I'm so silly. I talked about setting things clear and maintaining nothing but friendship. Look what almost happened for a third damn time.

Unbuckling his seatbelt, Micah lingers, catches his breath, and then looks at me. "You know, you didn't answer my question."

A sharp breath surges from my lips. "Why is my answer so important to you?"

"Maybe you don't," he concludes. "That's why it's so hard to say it."

I swallow hard and turn away from his stare as I lie, "I love Nate. We have a great relationship. Who knows, we might be together after college. That's why... what almost happened..." I carry my eyes back to him. "It can't happen again."

His eyes suddenly grow dark. His expression is intense, brooding.

Micah nods, regarding me intensely. "I was messing with you again. Don't be so worried. I wasn't going to kiss you."

Those words hurt along with his sly grin like our near kiss that would never be real meant nothing.

He hops out and shuts the door, bending at the window. "By the way, you're not a very good liar."

I scoff. "I'm not lying."

"Yeah, you are. If you loved him, you wouldn't have been out with me tonight. You wouldn't be deliberating it so much. That's why you would have let me kiss you."

He walks away, heading to the house. Before going inside, he looks back and adds, "You know what else? Anyone can see the truth in your eyes."

"What truth?" I call out.

"That you're not so sure about your relationship, no matter how you try to convince yourself it's great."

He steps inside before I can protest.

Jerk.

Micah reads me so easily. It's strange how we've only known each other for a few days, and he's already deciphered so much about me. But he's not a very good liar, either. I recognized that look in his eyes. Disappointment. I know it well.

I could tell Micah was going to kiss me tonight. He's right. I wanted him to at that moment.

And still do now.

Entering my room, I see the one person I don't want to face right now sprawled across my bed.

Claudia sits up with her back pushed against the headboard as I close the door and place my phone and keys on my dresser.

"Where've you been?" she asks. "You got off work almost two hours ago. Did you hang out with Nate?"

I kick off my flats and plop down on the chair. "No, mother. I went to Pure with Micah since I've been dying to listen to Allysen Callery, and I thought he'd enjoy her music, too."

She frowns. "Let me get this straight. You have a boyfriend, yet you hung out with a single man alone?" Accusation slices through her voice.

I perk up to defend myself, even though she has a point. "We were hanging out as friends. There's nothing wrong with that. I won't get in your way of dating him."

"Whatever," she huffs, chipping at her silver nail polish. "I'm not interested in Micah, anyway. He likes someone else."

Does he? My mind goes ballistic, wondering who she is, and at the same time, I'm mad at him for flirting with me when he already has someone he likes.

Easing off the chair, I walk over to my bed and plop down beside Claudia. I can feel the ocean breeze coming in through the open window. The night is starting to cool. Or maybe it's being near Micah earlier that had me so hot.

"Is everything okay?" I ask her, realizing she's not jealous of me being around him as I initially thought.

Claudia raises her shoulders and mumbles, "Ryan and Kimberly are going exclusive."

"And that's a problem because?"

"It's Ryan. He's too good for that bitch. Plus, she's a year older, and there's nothing sexier to a guy than a cougar."

Oh, that's right. How could I have forgotten that Claudia and Ryan dated briefly in junior high school? That was the longest relationship she'd ever had. I think it lasted four months. That's a record for her. She usually ditches guys by the third week, sometimes sooner.

"I'm sorry, Claudia," I say, squeezing her arm. "I didn't even realize you still liked him."

She pouts and combs back her wavy red strands, resting her head on my shoulder.

"If you wanted to be with him again, why didn't you tell him?"

"I tried to at the bonfire," she says. "Kimberly was all over him. She ensured Ryan and I didn't talk."

I squeeze her hand. "So, what do you want to do?"

"What do you mean? It's over. He's with her. Like, in a relationship for real now. They've been hooking up. Why would he leave a girl who gives it up to him for a girl who wouldn't? I never wanted to sleep with him when we were together."

That surprises me. "You never slept with Ryan? Then what was that talk about guys having needs, and if we don't take care of them, they'll wonder?"

She snorts. "You shouldn't listen to me sometimes. I mostly spew fuckery."

I bump her arm and lie down, resting my head on my pillow. "I couldn't sleep with Nate last night, either," I tell her.

"Really?" Claudia lies down next to me. "It's probably for the best."

"Why'd you say that?"

She nestles closer. "Um... I heard a girl talking shit last night. It could be gossip. I mean, you know how girls are—"

"What did she say?" I spring up, looking down at her.

Claudia drifts away from my gaze and stares at the curtain, swaying in the breeze. She has a taut look on her face.

"Tell me," I urge.

"All right," she caves. "She said one of her friends hooked up with Nate a few days ago."

She eyes me with a worried expression, checking to see if I'm okay. I'm not, but I sort of am. I should be fuming. I should find out who the girl is so I can do something childish like egg her car or house and call Nate to curse him out. But I don't want to do anything. Instead, I exhale deeply and fall onto my pillow again.

"Reign," Claudia says quietly. "I'm sure it's not true. Nate's loyal to you."

"It's true," I mutter, keeping my eyes closed. Do I even have a right to be mad when I wanted to kiss Micah so many times since he started working at Captain's Choice?

Turning onto my side, I flick the light off and whisper, "Goodnight."

Claudia doesn't utter anything about it, only says, "Goodnight."

After a long pause, she murmurs, "Reign, when I say I think Micah likes someone else..."

"Yeah?" I ask, though not wanting to hear more bad news.

"I think it's you."

That will keep me up all night because I'm starting to wonder if I like him, too.

NINETEEN

Micah

WELL, I'LL BE DAMNED! On my way out on Wednesday morning, I spot a bicycle leaning against the oak tree in front of the house. My landlord's looking to get rid of it. There's a paper with 'Free' stuck to the tree, so I walk over to check out the bike.

Except that the red artwork on the crossbar has worn, it doesn't look too bad. The tires and brakes seem to be in good condition. I knock on his door and tell him I'll take it off his hands. I was planning on getting a bike anyway, so this works.

As much as I like Reign offering to drive me home and steering off to other places, it'll make me feel less of a bother having the bike. I wonder if she'll consider riding on it with me. Yeah, right, that's if she was my girl. She's not. I need to stop making it hard for her.

As I pull up to Captain's Choice, place my bike around back, and walk inside, her beautiful face is the first to greet me, sending a rush of desire all over me. Since Monday night, she's been evading me.

Our almost kiss plays over and over in my head. I want it to happen so badly. I'm desperate for her touch. But I know it's not what she wants, and I need to stop trying to wreck her relationship.

While Reign's getting tables ready, I walk up to her and say jokingly, "You don't have to drive me home anymore. I'm no longer your burden."

She swivels and stares at me with her forehead creased. "You're not a burden. Did you get a car?"

"No, I got a bike instead."

"Oh, I see. Okay." She turns and continues what she was doing before.

"Reign," I mutter at her back.

Rotating again, she waits for me to say what's on my mind.

"I'm sorry I've been making you feel uncomfortable. I was only joking around at the bistro. It won't happen again."

"Okay." She plays with her hands and looks down at her feet as she utters, "Thanks."

"So, are we cool now? No more avoiding me?" I smile.

Reign smiles in return. "We're cool. It's nice you've gotten a bike, but you weren't a burden to me. I told you, I don't mind."

My grin expands. "Does that mean you want me to get rid of the bike and keep letting you offer me rides then?"

She angles her head to the side. "Gosh, you're just—"

"Charming?" I cut her off. "Irresistibly handsome?"

She can't fight back her laugh. "We should get some work done, Mr. Charming."

I nod. "Yes, ma'am."

Aislin strolls in the second I turn from Reign. She slows to a stop, studies us, and then rolls her eyes as she struts off. I guess she's remembering how close Reign and I were that time out back. She's cool, but damn her for interrupting us.

Throughout the day, dark clouds fill the sky. I hear an occasional rumble. But just my luck, it chooses to rain at closing. I look out the window, waiting for it to ease up, glimpsing Reign out of the corner of my eye. She has a sneaky smirk plastered on her pink lips as she waits by the door.

"What?" I ask.

"You want a ride?" she offers smartly, crossing her arms at her waist.

"That was the point in me getting the bike," I tell her, drawing closer.

"Well, a bike isn't convenient in these conditions. By the way, I checked the forecast, and there's a hundred percent chance it'll rain until tomorrow morning."

"Shit." I fold my arms, studying her face. "Why are you grinning?"

She straightens. "I'm not."

I give her the 'really?' stare, and she laughs. After a few seconds, she composes herself.

"I'm sorry. Leave your bike here for tonight, and I'll drive you home. It's not like you can ride it in the morning, either."

She does have a point, and who am I kidding? I love being close to this girl. "Okay, if you insist."

We run out to her car and hurry inside. Her hair's damp. It looks darker. Sexier. I turn away fast when she catches me staring. I need to try to stop doing that. She has a boyfriend. I'm making her feel uncomfortable.

Tonight, we go straight to my house. It sucks, but Mother Nature has other plans, and I'm not so sure Reign wants to hang out with me alone anymore.

I retrieve my keys from my pocket and prepare to run. Before I slide over to open the passenger door, she asks, "Can I see your apartment?"

Surprised and excited all at once, I spin to meet her gaze. She has no idea how much that question tickles my stomach. Having Reign inside my home makes me feel like a kid on Christmas morning.

I swallow a sudden burst of nerves and say calmly, "Sure. I'll head out first and unlock the door so you can hurry inside behind me."

She waits for me to do that, dashing through the rain into the building after. I lead her upstairs to the third floor and let her inside my spot. She looks around, taking it in.

"I like the layout," she says, glancing back at me.

"Yeah, it's all right," I say, shutting the door. I consider locking it to hold her my prisoner for the night.

"Want something to drink? Water? Soda?" I ask, walking over to the kitchenette.

"Oh, water, please."

I open the refrigerator and grab bottled water, bringing one to her. She takes the cap off, gulping down a few drops before checking out the place.

"If you leave in August, I could take this place off your hands," she suggests. Facing me again, she adds, "Did you have to sign a lease or anything?"

"Yeah, for the three months, but I'm considering extending it now," I tell her, gesturing for her to have a seat.

"So, you're staying in Newport then?" she asks, drinking some more as she sits on the couch.

I sit across from her in the armchair. "I'm considering it. Haven't made up my mind as of yet."

She bobs her head slowly. "Okay. I'm glad you like it here enough to consider staying."

"Yeah, I have you to thank for that," I say.

"It's the least I can do for a friend."

Friend? As much as I hate that word, I have no choice if it's all she wants. There's no coming out of that zone once I'm in, though. *But she has a boyfriend.* It's hard to remember when she's smiling at me like that.

I look around and swallow hard, trying to bury the lust from taking over because, shit, we're so alone. This is the perfect opportunity to continue what started Monday night. But yeah, she has that boyfriend of hers.

"What are you thinking about?" Reign asks.

"Hmm? Oh..." I snap out of my dirty thoughts and straighten. "You should probably get going. It's coming down out there."

"Oh wow, Micah, you sure want to get rid of me," she jokes, getting off the couch. "Was it something I said?"

It's just you. You're so damn hot. It's killing me that I can't touch you.

"Not at all," I reply. Frustrated, I comb my hand through my hair and explain, "I'm worried about you driving in this downpour."

She smiles and starts for the door. I walk over, opening it for her.

"Well, see you at work," she says softly, moving from the doorway.

"See you." I wave as she heads for the stairs, only to stop her again. "Oh hey."

Reign swivels. "Yeah?"

I step out and walk up to her. "I was thinking maybe we could run together in the mornings?"

"Oh..."

"I mean, it's something we both like to do, and I find it even more motivating when I'm running with someone else... You know, like friends."

She nods. "Sure."

"Also, can I get your number? Friends do that too, you know." I laugh.

"Silly, of course, I'll give you my number. No need to justify every little thing, Micah."

Taking her phone out of her pocket, Reign hands it to me, and I punch in my number. She calls my phone to save hers and proceeds on her way, waving with a sweet smile as she descends the stairs and leaves my sight.

God! Why can't this girl be mine?

TWENTY

Reign

JUNE FLEW BY so fast. We're in July now, and I'm starting to reconsider the trip to Florida with Claudia at the end of the month. I wonder if that has anything to do with Micah.

We've been running together for two weeks before work in the mornings. We'd meet near the beach, jog for half a mile, and return to the starting point as day breaks.

I'm noticing his muscles more than ever, especially since he sometimes runs without a shirt.

Summer's getting hotter, and so is he. I can't stop myself from watching every stream of sweat trickle down his chiseled chest as we collapse on the sand to catch our breaths and quench our thirsts.

His Adam's apple bobs as he chugs the rest of his water and lowers with his hands behind his head. As he closes his eyes and tries to recuperate, I sit there drinking in his masculine features. Even when sweaty and out of breath, Micah still looks so damn hot.

He squints at me and smirks cockily. I look away fast and continue to drink my water. I suspect he's been trying to seduce me, but maybe I'm thinking too much.

Shortly after, he sits up and observes the surfers pulling up to catch the morning waves. He bumps my shoulder and springs to his feet. "Let's go for a swim. We'll cool down faster."

I wave him off. "You go. I'll wait here."

Dropping his head to one side, Micah surveys me with narrowed eyes. "Are you afraid of swimming or something?" He looks back at the ocean. "You never want to go in."

I glance down at the sand and dig my sneakers into it. And before I can change my mind, I hear myself reveal, "My sister drowned when she was thirteen."

"Oh, wow. I'm so sorry, Reign." He lowers before me, lightly touching my arm. It incites a sensation I never knew I could experience.

"What was her name?" he asks.

I stare at his hand on my arm, so surprised by his touch that I find it hard to speak. Seeing my nervous reaction, Micah moves it away.

"Mary," I breathe out. "I was eleven when it happened. Didn't even scream for help. I saw her drowning and didn't do anything until it was too late." It's like I opened the floodgates and can't stop spilling everything.

Micah squeezes my shoulder, comforting me. "It's not your fault. You were a kid. You were in shock."

"They don't talk about her," I go on. "After Mary died, they took down her pictures, put her stuff in boxes, and piled them inside the garage. It's like she never existed."

"That was their way of coping," he tells me.

I turn my head and meet his gaze. Micah gently wipes a single tear from my cheek with his thumb.

"Oh, geez." I dip my face away from him, suppressing the rest of my tears. "I'm sorry. I'm being dramatic."

"You're not. Don't apologize. And it shouldn't be like that for your family," he says. "You shouldn't try to forget Mary. You should hold on to her memories. Work on moving from the pain while keeping her in your hearts. She'd want you to."

He lowers his eyes to the sand. I wonder how much of what he said refers to his own life.

"Tell me about your family," I say. "They must miss you. Do you have any brothers or sisters back in Colorado?" It hits me that he's barely said anything about himself since he's been here.

Micah stares at the ocean, watching the surfers attempt to ride waves. They aren't doing too well out there.

"I only had my grams," he whispers. "My dad came around now and then but finally stopped after I turned seventeen. So, no parents. I don't have any siblings, either."

He seems so far in his thoughts. I wish I could reach him there.

My mind repeats what Micah said. He *had* a grandmother but no one else.

"I'm sorry about your loss," I mutter, hoping he'll tell me more since I just shared losing my sister and the guilt I feel over her drowning.

After a brief pause, he says in a low tone, "She wasn't well for a while, and then something happened..." His voice trails. I can tell by the look on his face that he's hesitant to say more. "Anyway, Grams died. She was the only one I had, so I've been alone since."

"You're not alone," I utter, touching his back. "You have a friend."

Micah looks at me for a moment, disappointment in his eyes as he hops to his feet and pulls me up. In no time, a wide grin appears again as if he didn't say anything at all.

"Promise me something," he says sweetly.

"What?"

"That you'll go swimming with me before summer ends."

I consider his request long and hard. It'll take a lot of courage to walk into the water and not freak out, but Micah's right. It's time to let it go.

"Okay," I say bravely. "Promise."

I find Nate leaning against his Porsche when I head outside. He has his arms folded tightly across his chest while glaring at me.

"What's going on?" he asks as I draw closer.

"What do you mean?"

Unfolding his arms, he straightens and strokes my cheek. "Babe, you've been so cold for the past few days.

You don't want to hang out, and you don't return my calls. What's up with you?"

I shrug. "It's not that I don't want to hang out. I'm busy with work." The truth is I have been contemplating the future of our relationship. If we even have one.

"That's always your excuse," he hisses. Eyeing the restaurant over my shoulder, he asks, "Aren't you going to stop working now, as you've promised? What about the Florida trip?"

Why is he bringing that up when Claudia and I decided to go? Nate already said he wasn't coming because of other plans, which baffles me since he didn't go on our graduation trip to the Bahamas, claiming that he stayed behind for me.

I don't believe that anymore.

"I'm still thinking about it. My mom could use my help," I tell him. "Business is unpredictable, especially since that other seafood restaurant opened."

Annoyed, he cuts his eyes away from me. "Gosh, your mom needs a thicker skin if she wants to stay in this business."

I look at him open-mouthed, stunned by his remark. Nate doesn't stop sharing his opinion. With no regard for my feelings, he continues, "She should come up with ways to attract more customers and improve that boring menu, not complain about competitors. There are plenty more restaurants around here, so she should suck it up and raise the bar if she wants to be in with the big boys."

Backing up a few steps, I drop my hands and snap at him, "Excuse me?"

Nate narrows his eyes, staring at me blankly as if he didn't say anything wrong. "What?"

"*What*? Nate, you bashed my mother's business skills and don't seem to care that you're being rude and out of line."

He throws his hands up. "That's not out of line. I meant it in the nicest way possible. She seriously needs to consider upgrading the restaurant."

Noticing that I'm still upset with him, Nate reaches for my arm. I move away.

"Babe," he scoffs. "You're not mad, are you?"

I pivot on my heels and start for my car, seeing Micah exit the restaurant. He avoids looking at us as he stops at his bike.

Nate hurries up to me, grasps my arms, and turns me to face him. "What's really going on here?"

"What are you talking about?" I hiss.

"I'm talking about you being all distant ever since that night. Even though I said it's fine and that we can wait, you're still acting as if I'm pressuring you about sex."

I flick to Micah, thinking he might have heard that. He shakes his head in amazement and starts to leave, walking off with his bike instead of riding away.

Squirming from Nate's grip, I unlock my car and open the door. He slams it shut before I get in and braces himself against it.

"Tell me what's bothering you so we can fix it because you're upset with me for whatever reason."

I say in a calm tone, "Nate, can you move, please? I'm tired and don't feel like talking. I want to go home."

134

His eyes widen, seeming icy. "No. We need to talk right now, Reign. You might lose me completely if you don't tell me what's on your mind. Not many guys can tolerate your hot and cold personality, so you might end up alone for the rest of your life if you let me go."

"Hey!"

We both glance at Micah, surprised. He lowers his bike to the ground and steps forward while glaring at Nate. "Why don't you save her the trouble and take yourself out of her life? She can obviously do better."

I quickly reach for Nate's arm as he turns to face Micah. From the bulging veins in his neck, the situation is becoming intense. They might end up fighting.

Over me.

A part of me can't help feeling a rush from that, but the sensible part knows not to let it continue.

"Who the hell do you think you are?" Nate fires at him. "Why don't you mind your damn business, get on your little bicycle, and ride along."

Micah chuckles in return. "Actually, I don't have to do that since your girlfriend loves driving me."

Oh God.

I bite my lip when Nate glances back at me, a combination of anger and jealousy etched on his face.

"Who can blame her when she has a boyfriend like you," Micah adds fuel to the flames.

Nate snaps his head to him, brushes off my hand, and marches over to Micah. I hurry behind him. He straightens in his face and grunts his next words. "I've noticed the way you hang around Reign, trying to weasel your piece of shit self into her life. Listen good, asshole. Stay the fuck away from my girlfriend, or I'll make your life a living hell."

Laughing it off with his usual carefree self, Micah glances at me and looks back at Nate, saying confidently, "Open your eyes, dude. She doesn't want me to stay away from her."

True.

I squeeze in between them as Nate grabs for Micah's shirt. I press my hand against his chest and ease him back, looking from one to the other. "Both of you, stop it." I focus on Micah, telling him calmly, "Please go."

Confusion morphs his face like he expected me to say that to Nate instead. I can't. Nate's my boyfriend. Not Micah. I need to remember that.

I turn away to avoid the sad look in his eyes. The next thing I hear is his bike taking off and Nate scoffing. "What a loser. He can't even afford a damn car."

"Why does that make him a loser?" I counter, defending Micah.

Nate looks at me hard, suspicion still in his eyes. "Why were you driving him home? Is that why you couldn't hang out with me after work? You were busy playing chauffeur to that bum."

"That's enough!" I yell. "I wasn't hanging out with you because you're always hounding me for sex."

"Oh, stop being so dramatic," he fires back. "If I wanted sex that bad, I could get any other girl to give it up to me—"

"Wow. The truth comes out." I step past him and head to my car, hoping this time he'll let me leave.

Only he follows me again. "Reign, wait."

Sliding onto the seat, I slam the door shut, turn the key in the ignition, and put on my seatbelt.

Nate arches at the window, tapping on it. I keep it up more than halfway so he can't stick his hand inside to try and turn off the car.

"C'mon, don't be like this," he implores.

"Is it true?" I finally ask.

He throws his hands up frustratingly. "Is what true?"

"That you cheated on me?" I glare at him.

His face drops, and he backs away from the car, twitching his mouth. His sudden quiet answers my question.

Silence is admittance.

Before pulling out of the parking lot, I ask, "Do I know her?"

He's unable to meet my gaze. "No. It was a mistake. I was drunk. She was there..." He looks up again, saying, "I'm sorry, baby."

"Screw you."

I drive off, leaving him in the parking lot of Captain's Choice with his hands on his head, fuming.

He doesn't jump into his Porsche and follow me home. He's not the one texting me an hour later, as I lie in bed and think about our relationship from the day it started till now, wondering why I ever decided to go out with him. He's also not the one outside my bedroom window now, hoping I'll come down.

Micah is. He showed up ten minutes after I texted him my address.

TWENTY-ONE

Micah

"THIS IS NICE," Reign says in a breathy tone as we sit on a grassy hilltop looking down at Newport Harbor. I wasn't expecting her to come out tonight. After all, she was upset with me for saying all that stuff to Nate.

But when I glimpsed the look in her eyes as she snuck out her front door and hurried over to me, I knew I was in the clear. I even got her to hop up on my bike so I could ride her out to this spot.

"I didn't even know about this," she tells me, smiling as she meets my gaze.

"That's an ego boost for me." I grin. "It's cool knowing something about Newport that you don't."

We continue staring at the ocean and stars. There are not too many to look at tonight, though.

"I'm sorry," I tell her. "I shouldn't have said anything. I shouldn't have gotten involved."

When she drops her head and looks at me, I add, "I'm sorry I caused trouble for your relationship."

"You've been doing that ever since you came here," she says.

"I know, and I'm—"

"Sorry?" She smiles. "You've said that so many times."

"It's just..."

"Just what?" She leans her head to one side, her gorgeous hazel eyes darkened by the night. The shade is so embedded in my head that I can even envision their sparkle.

It's now or never. I have to come out and tell her the truth. "I lied back at *Pure*. I wasn't messing with you, Reign. I wanted to kiss you. I've wanted to kiss you since I saw you in the park." I pause to let her soak in my words. She keeps her eyes steady on me, never looking away. That motivates me to continue confessing. "I like you, Reign. I like you a lot. And I know it's wrong to interfere with your relationship, and I've tried to put you out of my head, but I can't. I'm too damn attracted to you. I can tell you're not happy with that guy."

She's still quiet, looking at me with an unreadable expression. I wish she'd say something, anything.

Slap me. Let me know you've heard everything.

"Choose me," I let slip out. "Let me be the one to make you happy." I probably seem so damn desperate. I don't care. She needs to know how I feel about her.

Finally, Reign catches her breath and mutters softly, "I shouldn't be here with you. Shouldn't be around you. I don't know why I let it get this far... I don't think we should even be friends."

Seriously?

My stomach sinks. That's all she can say after I spilled my guts to her? I'm practically lifeless here. My

139

heart's in my hands. I'm willing to give it all to her. I've never done that before.

Ever.

"Um... So... You don't feel the same way?" I ask, feeling like a complete idiot.

Reign pushes to her feet and brushes off her jeans and blouse. She shakes her head and tells me in a shaky tone, "I don't know what I'm feeling right now."

I stand. Before I can utter another word, she steps past me to my bike, indicating she wants to leave. I suppress the hurt to take her home with a clear mind.

As we approach her beach house, I slow down a little from the fence in case her parents are awake and see her coming back with me at this hour.

Reign hops off the bike and lingers in place. She chips at her nails, asking, "Will you be okay?"

"Yeah," I answer dryly, looking ahead. "Go inside before your parents find you missing and freak out."

When our eyes meet, excitement consumes me. My heart hammers. Fire ignites in my stomach. I can see all she's trying to hide. Her emotions are beyond clear.

"I'll see you tomorrow," she says coolly.

Reign turns and starts toward her gate. I spring from my bike, hurry to her, and grip her arm. Turning her to face me, I wrap my arms around her curvy frame, bringing her in close—closer than we've ever been. She doesn't pry out of my grasp, confirming my suspicion. "You do feel the same way."

She gasps as I press my mouth to her soft lips, kissing her hard to make up for all the missed opportunities. Reign tips her head and clutches my lower back, squeezing me as she parts her lips to deepen the kiss. I tighten my hold on her, caressing her body and running my fingers through her long hair. She smells incredible—a mixture of berries and vanilla. But she tastes even better as our tongues lock, and I drown myself in the candy flavor of her mouth.

An intense moan rushes from her lips as I start to kiss her neck. Reign trails her hands all over my body, aggressively caressing me.

She's so warm. She feels so damn good! I can't control the bulge in my jeans with her pressed into me like this. I've never wanted any girl as badly as I want Reign. The tension has been building since we met. Now, I feel as if I'm about to explode.

"Come home with me," I hear myself beg. "Please."

She groans before breaking out of my grasp. I steady my breathing and reach a hand out to her. With no hesitation, Reign takes it and guides me toward her car. We're almost there when her phone vibrates.

I want to smash it into pieces when she pulls it out of her pocket. She stares at the screen, saying almost breathlessly, "It's my mom. She's wondering where I am."

Just like that, our night together is over.

"I have to go inside," she murmurs, nodding to the front door.

I need to get out of here before her mom catches us together. "Want to meet in the morning?"

She looks frightened by my question, so I clarify, even though I don't understand why, "I mean to go running before work."

Peering at the ground, she answers without meeting my gaze, "Maybe not. I need to think all this through."

"Okay." I shift closer to kiss her cheek, but she turns.

Reign reaches her front door, slipping inside without looking back.

"Good night," I whisper to myself.

With a long breath, I walk back to my bike and look up at the house, hoping Reign isn't regretting our moment of passion. It would rip me apart if she pretended it never happened and resumed her relationship with Nate when that was the best kiss I've ever experienced. Ever!

TWENTY-TWO

Reign

I RELEASE the breath I've been holding the second I enter my house. Frick! That kiss was fire! I've never felt the way I do now after kissing Nate. It feels so much different, so much better.

"Where'd you go?" Mom asks, peeking out of her bedroom the moment I reach upstairs.

"Next door," I lie. "Claudia's upset. Boy stuff."

She bobs her head slowly. "I'm sure she'll return to her charismatic self soon. Just try not to stay out this late after work, Reign."

I smile at her, and she returns to her room. I walk to mine, plopping down on my bed after closing the door. My whole body is boiling over with heat. If Mom hadn't texted me, I certainly would've gone to Micah's house and let him have me.

Funny how I've been apprehensive about sex all this time, then suddenly, Micah comes along, and I want to toss my virginity at him.

I hope he's not upset that I couldn't run with him in the morning. I need to sort out everything and make a decision. If I want to end whatever is between us before it grows deeper or break it off with Nate. I'm weighing heavily toward ending things with the latter since he's cheated on me. Then again, aren't I doing the same thing?

I barely had any decent sleep. Of course, that's nothing new. Only this time, I stayed up replaying the steamy kiss and what I'll do today.

The moment light encapsulates my room, I climb out of bed, take a quick shower, and dress in black jeans and a sleeveless top, putting on my flats before snatching my phone from the dresser and tiptoeing downstairs.

Mom and Dad aren't up. I amble through the kitchen and sneak out the side door, crossing the lawn to Claudia's house. Hopefully, she'll forgive me when I tell her Micah and I kissed because I need her advice.

Approaching the glass door, I see Ms. Norman in the kitchen, cleaning before she starts breakfast. I tap on the door and wave. She wrinkles her brows as she strolls over to let me in.

"Good morning, Ms. Norman," I greet politely.

She inclines her head as she replies, "Morning, dear. It's so early. You know that friend of yours isn't up yet."

"I know, but I wanted to discuss something important before work. You mind if I run upstairs?"

Mrs. Norman pats my arm lightly. "You know you don't have to ask. Go on."

Climbing the stairs, I quietly open Claudia's bedroom door and enter. I walk over and shake her arm to wake her.

"Hmm... go away, Eleanor," she groans.

"It's not your stepmother," I chuckle.

Turning over, Claudia squints at me and buries her face back into the pillow. "Reign, do you have any idea what time it is?"

I sit on the side of the bed. "I know, but I need to talk to you about this."

She pushes up and throws her messy hair out of her face. "What is it?" she asks, rubbing her eyes.

"First, promise me you won't be mad."

Claudia dips her head and stares down her nose at me as if I'm being silly. "You know I'll never be mad at you."

"Okay." I exhale deeply and reveal, "Micah and I kissed last night."

"Whoa!" She's certainly awake now.

"I know. I tried to fight my attraction to him all this time, but then we started running together, and it became harder. Now I don't know what to do."

"Hold up! Wait a sec." She slithers down beside me, "You've been running in the mornings with Micah, and you kept it a secret from me?"

I purse my lips and frown while nodding.

"Okay, I'm jealous that you get the chance to sweat with that hot stud muffin, but this is not about me."

She slaps me on the arm.

"Ow! What was that for?"

"Reign! Open your eyes! Why are you in my room moping, talking about not knowing what to do? You should be with Micah now, kissing at sunrise and doing delectable things with him."

"But..." I hop off the bed and pace the room. "There's Nate—"

"Forget about him!" Claudia springs to her feet. "He's just a cheating dickbag, anyway." She squeezes my arms. "What's the problem? It's obvious who you want to be with; your eyes are glowing so much right now because of Micah."

"I'm scared of all I feel for him. Not to mention, he's probably not staying in Newport after August. And there's so much I still don't know about him."

"Geez, stop being so analytical. How about you give it one day at a time? For now, enjoy each other. Don't worry so much about perfection, Reign. What you need to do is set it straight with Nate. Tell him you've fallen for someone else because you have."

She giggles and jerks my arms. I throw them around her, hugging her tightly. "You're not mad about Micah?"

"Of course not." She eases me out to look me in the eye. "I told you, he likes *you*. I never had a chance, and I certainly won't get in between you two." Twisting me around, Claudia smacks my butt and shoves me towards her room door. "Now go, you have one to dump and another to do business with." She giggles. "Choices, choices."

"All right, see you later," I say as I open the door.

"Text me the juicy details, or better yet, snap me a pic of you and Micah together."

"Bye, Claudia." I roll my eyes and step outside, heading from her house to the beach where I hopefully have a sexy new boyfriend waiting for me.

TWENTY-THREE

Micah

THE FIRST sunrise you see after a passionate kiss is so much different from the ones you glimpse on any other day. You're more motivated to stop and stare.

Even though Reign told me she wouldn't be coming out for a run this morning, like a fool, I still jogged down to the beach and waited for her.

I had a feeling in my gut last night, and when I opened my eyes earlier, I thought today would be a great day for me. But she's usually here before daybreak, and the dark clouds have already moved, giving way to the blazing sun. I have to drill it into my head that she's not coming for real.

Sulking, I twirl around to head home. That's when I see the familiar radiant face and sparkly eyes smiling back at me. I stop instantly. An air of relief surges from my lips.

"Hey," she says, her voice sounding sweeter than ever. My heart begins to pound so much I fear it'll leave dents in my chest.

Reign slowly walks to me in the sand, her olive skin beaming in the sun. "How's it going?"

"*How's it going?*" I repeat in a playful tone, folding my arms. "Not so good. Let's see, I slept like crap last night because you told me you had some stuff to think about, and you didn't even want to go running with me this morning. So I'm bummed out that you didn't get to admire my body earlier drenched in sweat."

She beams at my pouty face and edges closer, tipping in her sneakers to kiss my cheek. Then she drapes her arms around my neck and breathes, "I'm sorry. There's nothing to think about. I want to be with you, Micah."

I ease her away to confirm what she said. "You mean you *really* want to be with me?"

"Yes," she says with a laugh. "I do."

Elated, I yank her into my chest and kiss her hungrily, reenacting the moment of passion from last night.

Though no other kiss could outdo our first, the feeling remains. It's even deeper. Reign stays in my grasp for several long seconds before finally backing away to catch her breath. A broad smile spreads across her face. It melts my heart.

"Did you tell him?" I have to know. That's the only way she'll assure me she's with me now.

My stomach plunges when she shakes her head and mutters, "No. Not yet."

Noticing the excitement is gone from my face, she quickly adds, "I'll tell him later, after work."

"Sure," I say. "I can't expect you to change everything for me in only a couple of hours."

Hooking her arm around mine, Reign leads me up the beach towards her car.

"Wanna hang out later?" I ask her. "That singer is back in town. The one you like. Allysen... something."

She giggles before saying, "Allysen Callery, and yes, I'd love to hang out."

"Cool. It'll be our first official date then."

Turning her head down, Reign tries to hide her blushing cheeks. She smiles innocently and tightens her grip on me. I nuzzle her closer to my side, kissing the top of her head.

"You're so cute," I tell her.

She pushes me teasingly and dashes ahead while shouting over her shoulder, "Last one to the car buys breakfast!"

"Yeah, right!" I yell back, jogging behind her. Reign leans against the door, a smug grin on her lips.

"Even though you cheated," I say, pressing against her, "it's not like I'd let you buy me breakfast."

She locks her fingers around my neck. "Well, what if I wanted to treat you?"

"I can think of other ways you could treat me," I tease.

Suddenly, her face tenses, and she slowly loosens her hands from around my neck, switching to an awkward mood as she messes with the door. "We should go," she says. "So we'll have enough time to eat before work."

"Yeah."

I move around to the passenger side and hop in. Reign lingers a moment before getting in as well.

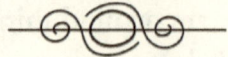

Reign and I drown ourselves in another passionate make-out session after breakfast. Then she drops me off at my house so we can get to work separately.

After showering, I haul on a gray shirt and blue jeans. My phone rings as I step outside and close the door. I assume it's Pete calling to convince me to talk to Ashley again. When I look at the screen, I see Greg's name.

My stomach tenses. I stop midstride on the stairs, considering whether I should answer. Now that I'm starting to feel happy again, I don't want any reminders of Haxtun.

Sliding the phone inside my pocket, I hurry downstairs, take out my bike, and ride to work.

I arrive at the restaurant shortly and park my bike around back. My phone starts to ring again as I'm about to enter. Damn, Greg's not giving up. I finally answer to get it over with.

"What's up, Greg?" I feign interest.

"Mitchel, it's been a while." Concern laces his usual cheerful voice.

"Not long enough," I grumble. "You said you'd let me breathe." My voice sounds harsh.

Greg exhales long and hard before saying, "He's awake, Mitchel. Lewis Harrison is finally awake."

After a few seconds, I find my voice again, muttering, "He is?"

"His wife called me. She found out I was your counselor in juvie and wanted me to set up a meeting," he explains. "They've been looking for you. Lewis wants to see you. You have to come back to Haxtun."

My stomach drops. There's no way I can go back. No way will I see his family or him. I'm too ashamed. I can't face them.

"You know I can't," I tell Greg.

"Mitchel, you have to stop running. We both know it wasn't your fault, and Lewis wants you to know that, too. The man's out of his coma after two years, and he's asking for you. You owe it to him."

"Tell him..." I pause, not sure what to say. "Look, just give me some time."

"Mitchel, I think—"

"I need time, Greg," I say again and hang up.

I'm glad Lewis Harrison woke up from his coma, but I'm partly to blame for putting him in that situation. He's missed two years with his wife and son. How can I look at them? How can I look at *him*?

Frustration must be stamped on my face when I tread inside the restaurant because Aislin asks, "You okay?"

"Yeah... I'm fine." I walk past her to the back room and change into a uniform.

I should return to Haxtun and face Lewis. It's the right thing to do. Grams would have wanted me to. But I feel like a coward. I can't do it alone.

My body shudders when I feel Reign's arms wrap around me from behind. I clasp my hands over hers and take a breather.

"Your mom might see this," I say.

She tightens her grip and rests her head against my back. "I should tell her, anyway. Besides, I wanted to steal a hug before you came out because you seemed so off. You didn't even say hi when you showed up earlier. Walked right by me to change."

It is time to tell her about Haxtun. I've been hiding it in my heart long enough, and Reign could be the one to give me the courage I need to return.

Loosening her arms, I turn to face her. "Listen, uh, about Haxtun—"

Voices interrupt me before I spill the truth. Her mom and a man in a dress shirt and formal pants walk by the room. Mrs. Aldridge notices us and backtracks, peering into the room with a scowl.

"What's going on?" she asks suspiciously.

"Who was that?" Reign counters.

Mrs. Aldridge dawdles for a fraction of a second, then says, "That was Dean Carmichael. He's a friend and a restaurant broker."

Reign straightens in her amazement. "A broker? Why is he here?"

"We'll talk about it later," she says before disappearing in the passage.

I touch Reign's shoulders and knead out her sudden tension. "What's going on with your mom?"

She shrugs. "I don't know. Think she's planning on selling after summer."

"I'm sorry, babe."

Twisting, she smiles at me. "Babe? Hmm, I like that. It sounds good when you say it."

I'll tell her about Lewis and what happened in Haxtun when I decide to return. Right now, I want to enjoy what's starting between us and not think about anything else.

TWENTY-FOUR

Reign

I'M ABOUT TO CALL Nate when I step out of the restaurant, only to see him waiting for me in the parking lot. He looks pitiful with sad eyes and a dull face.

Building the courage to tell him the truth, I push myself forward, saying, "Nate, I was going to call you. Look, I'm—"

"Baby, I'm so sorry." He hurries up to me and tugs me into his embrace. "I never meant to hurt you. It was a stupid mistake. I promise it'll never happen again."

I wrench myself out of his arms and try again. "Nate, there's something I have to tell you. I—"

"Let's go to our special place and talk," he interrupts me as if he knows what's on my mind. "We'll have more privacy."

Something sinks in me when I look into his eyes and see the anticipation. I feel guilty for breaking up with him, but it's something I must do. I can't have a relationship with him when I want to be with Micah. It's not fair to either of them.

Nate pulls me to his car before I say anything else. Maybe going with him will help him deal with the breakup better. It's probably good that way. We'll end where we began.

He opens the passenger door for me and hurries into the driver's side, backing out of the parking lot.

Just my luck, Micah exits the restaurant the instant Nate pulls onto the road. He sees me in my boyfriend's car, and a dark shadow crosses his face.

Oh yeah, he's pissed.

We arrive at our spot at the beach and sit on the rocks. I keep fiddling with my phone in case Micah calls or texts me. We're supposed to hang out tonight, and I'm trying to hurry up the process to go back and explain it to him. But Nate won't stop talking about the first time he saw me in high school and how he finally decided to ask me out too late.

"I shouldn't have waited so long," he says. "Telling you how I felt two months before we graduated was stupid when I wanted to do it way before. We would've gotten to know each other so much more."

"It's fine," I tell him, rubbing my thumb across the phone screen.

"What's up with you and your phone?" he asks, annoyed.

I put it in my pocket and meet his gaze. There's no easy way to do this. Better to just come out and say it. "Nate, um... I'm sorry, but we should stop seeing each other."

He knits his brows together. "What? You want us to break up?"

"Yes," I reply in a whisper. "I don't think we're working and—"

"I said I'm sorry, Reign. People make mistakes. It won't happen again."

"It's not about you cheating. I'm not even as upset about it as I ought to be, and that only means I don't really want to be with you."

"Wow," he scoffs, amazed by my remark. Nate throws his head back and glances up at the starry sky. A minute passes before he looks at me again. "So, just like that, we're done? Do you even care that you're hurting me right now? When did you become so inconsiderate of my feelings?"

"I'm sorry," I say. "It's not that I'm inconsiderate; I just want to move on. And so should you."

Spinning away from his angry expression, I look out at the dark ocean as violent foam-topped waves rush to the shore; with every inhale, the salty sea breeze fills my nose. I can hear Mary's cries echo in the distance. She's out there, in the deep, waiting for me.

"You never even asked why I don't like boats or why I never go swimming," I say, my voice sounding faint.

He snorts before replying, "Because I always thought you didn't *want* to tell me."

Meeting his eyes again, I say, "That's just it. I don't feel like I can tell you things, not about Mary or my guilt."

Nate scrunches up his face and shakes his head. "Who the hell's Mary?"

"My sister," I answer in a whispery tone.

He furrows a brow. "I never knew you had a sister."

"Of course you did. Everyone here knows about the Aldridge girl who drowned. It was even on the news."

He throws his hands up. "See, that's what I don't like about you, Reign. You expect me to know stuff when you never bring anything up. Like how I'm supposed to know you're uncomfortable having sex when you're already letting me touch you all over."

I spring to my feet, upset. "It always comes back to sex with you. And the only reason I didn't tell you about my sister is because I know you'll call me crazy if I tell you I see her in the ocean, even though it's been seven years since she drowned."

With his mouth slightly open, Nate looks at me like a deer in headlights. "You see your dead sister?" There's a glint of ridicule in his voice. He's judging me.

Turning around, I start to head back, my feet heavy with every trek in the sand. I'm mad I shared something like that with him. What was the point, anyway? We're over.

"Where are you going?" he calls after me.

"I'm calling Claudia to pick me up," I fume over my shoulder.

He chases after me and reaches for my elbow, slowing me down. Whisking me around, he pulls me into his chest and hugs me tightly. "I'm sorry. I don't think you're crazy. I can't believe you never told me something like that, though." His voice has a softer edge now. "It's okay, Reign."

"It's not," I tell him, feeling empty in his embrace.

Gently, he eases me back. "Don't be like this, baby. You're only mad at me. I'll give you some time to clear your head, and we can start fresh. You can tell me more about Mary, and we'll... work on it together." There's uncertainty in the last part.

"No, Nate." I wring out of his grasp. "I don't need time to clear my head. I don't want to start fresh."

"But we love each other," he says harshly, his jaw tightening. I glance at his hands and notice his clenched fists.

His anger scares me. But I need to be honest with him. I need to tell Nate how I truly feel. "I'm sorry, but... I don't love you. Don't think I ever have. I thought that in time, I'd grow to care about you the way you say you care about me, but it never happened. I can't give you what you want, Nate. I'm so sorry. I really am."

The silence stretches without his response as he stares at me in the most disappointed way while breathing heavily.

Mary's voice still reverberates in the background amid the crashing waves and the loud beating of my heart. When I'm with Micah, she doesn't make a sound, yet when I'm alone or with anyone else, especially Nate, I hear her panicked screams.

I never understood why she wanted to swim so late that night. Then again, that was impulsive Mary, always doing crazy things.

"Fine," Nate sputters angrily, stepping past me. "I'll take you back to your car."

I pause to steady my nerves before following him. It's bad enough that I broke up with him, but now he has to drive me back.

What a killer.

When we return to *Captain's Choice*, Micah's bike is gone. Of course. But Mom's car is there in the parking lot. I get out of Nate's car and close the door, bending down at the window.

"I'm really sorry," I tell him again.

A smirk appears on his face as he glances over at me. "Sure you are." He revs his engine for me to back away. As soon as I do, he speeds off.

Sighing, I start over to the entrance, sending Micah a text as I unlock the door and step inside.

Me: Hey, sorry about tonight.

He replies not long after.

Micah: I'm over it. Have fun with your bf.

What does that mean? Is he no longer interested in me?

Me: Not with him. I'm back at CC.
R u home? I'll come over.

Micah: Don't need to.
Besides, it's going to rain.
U should head home.

Great. He's obviously mad at me. There's no way I'll drive home now.

"Thought you left?" Mom says, coming around the corner with her bag and a folder of papers.

"I wanted to tell you that I'm hanging out with Claudia for a while," I lie.

She shifts to one side and purses her lips. "You mean go to some party and spend the night at her house?"

"Yes..." I continue to lie, hoping she'll realize that I'm eighteen and shouldn't bar me from enjoying my youth. But if she says okay, does it mean I'm going to sleep over at Micah's? Am I truly ready for that after just ending one relationship?

There's a hesitant look on her already stressed face. Her forehead crinkles, and her eyes narrow. "I don't know about that, Reign."

I start to explain, "Mom—"

"I don't like the sound of you partying," she cuts me off. "You'll be starting college soon, and I don't want you falling into some terrible habit."

"But Mom, it's not like that."

"Whatever the case," Her razor-sharp voice conquers mine, "I think you should just drive home behind me and go to bed. Claudia doesn't have work tomorrow. You do."

Not hearing another word, she steps past me and pushes the door open. Mom waits for me to walk outside so that she can lock up. I guess I'm not going to see Micah tonight, then.

Stepping out of the shower, I haul on a long T-shirt, turn off the light, and slide under the covers. It started to rain shortly after we reached home, and now it's pouring outside.

I can't close my eyes without seeing Micah's face or remembering his text. All I want is to tell him why I left with Nate. Rolling over on my side, I reach for my phone and send him a text.

Me: Sleeping?

A minute passes without him answering, and I figure he's fast asleep. As I place the phone back on the side table, it buzzes. When I glance at the screen and see his message, my heart starts to race.

Micah: No. Guess I'm still waiting for u like a fool.

I get out of bed fast and put on a pair of jeans, a peach top, and my hoodie. I grab my keys and sneakers. It's the second time this guy has me sneaking out of my house in the middle of the night, but gosh, he's so worth it. There's a desire in my heart for him that I can't deny. The feeling is intense. It only grows deeper by the day.

So, here I am now, tiptoeing downstairs in the dark. I bite my lower lip and peek over my shoulder, hoping Mom and Dad don't hear me as I slip out the side door.

Huge droplets of rain hit my head and face as I step outside my house. I don't care. I'm going to Micah's apartment, and I'm ready for whatever happens next.

TWENTY-FIVE

Micah

THE SOUND of heavy rainfall beating against my window reminds me of the night Reign was here. And like an idiot, I touch the spot on the couch where she sat, pretending as if I'm touching her instead. I lean over and sniff the cushion. Surprisingly, her fragrance still lingers there.

"Shit!" I fume and run my hands through my hair.

This is absurd. She obviously made her choice and is reconsidering leaving Nate. No wonder she took off with him tonight.

It was stupid to believe she'd drop her boyfriend for me. Who am I kidding? He shows up, and without a second thought, she jumps into the car with him. I don't know why I even told her I was up waiting for her. She isn't coming. Not in this downpour, anyway.

I snatch the remote from the coffee table and flip through the channels, trying to preoccupy my mind with something else besides Reign. But when I'm not thinking about her, it's Lewis Harrison that haunts my mind, along with the fear of going back to Haxtun.

I pause on MTV, where an episode of *Ridiculousness* is on. Not too long ago, I became addicted to the show. My interest withered as someone just as risky popped into my life.

Jason wasn't like me. We were complete opposites. I was the good kid who never got in trouble. He was the definition of it. Yet I wanted to be his friend. I wanted to give him a chance because no one else would. Like me, Jason felt neglected by his parents. I should've seen there was no helping him. What the hell was I thinking?

Loud, urgent knocks at the door pull me out of my thoughts. My heart begins to pound behind my ribcage.

She really came. Reign's here.

I hurry over to the door and yank it open.

"Hey," she waves, worry cutting through her voice.

I lean on one leg and rest my hand on the door jamb, taking in her appearance. Her hair is soaking wet. Water streams down the side of her face. The thin blouse inside her drenched hoodie sticks to her body so much that the print on her bra is showing through.

Damn, she's sexy. A part of me wonders if she wittingly went dancing in the rain to come over here and taunt me.

"You're crazy," I say, shaking my head. "You came all the way here, in the middle of the night, not to mention in the pouring rain, just to see me?"

I keep my voice calm, pretending that her standing in my doorway so drenched doesn't wake up the animal in me.

Wiping water from her forehead, she replies, "I wanted to explain."

"Yeah?" I crumple my brows as I regard her.

"I came to tell you I'm sorry, Micah, and to explain why I left with Nate when you and I had plans. I just wanted to end things peacefully with him. If I'd broken up with Nate outside of the restaurant, he would have gone after you because he'd think it had something to do with you."

Sighing deeply, I stick my hands inside the pockets of my sweatpants. "Oh, so it doesn't have anything to do with me then?"

She wobbles her head. "It does."

What am I doing? She's standing in my doorway, shivering. Snapping out of my jealous mode, I quickly tow her inside and shut the door.

Reign keeps her back turned, speaking in a breathy voice. "It has everything to do with you." Spinning to face me, she adds, "I've never felt this way about anyone. Not even Nate. That's why I broke up with him, Micah."

She moves closer to me, placing her hand against my hammering heart. "I probably would've ended things even if you hadn't walked into my life, but I'm so glad you're here because I feel like I haven't really been living until I met you. That's why I'm standing here now. Like I said this morning, Micah, I want to be with you. I want you."

Her eyes are like fire, burning with lust. Desperation to touch her consumes me.

I cross the little distance and peel off her hoodie. I drape my arms around her soaked body, kissing her hard. Reign pushes into me. I sweep my tongue across her moist lips until she parts them and lets me slide inside.

The sweetness of her mouth stimulates the heat growing below my waist. I squeeze her body, wanting more. My insides coil with desire, and I feel as if I can't wait any longer.

I lower my hands beneath her butt, picking her up. Reign loops her legs around my waist and hooks her hands around my neck. I carry her to the bed. We continue kissing as I gently place her down. Her clothes are making my sheets wet, but I don't give a damn.

She moans and trembles when I climb over her. It has to be what we both want. I need to make sure.

"Tell me to stop," I breathe, stroking her beautiful face and brushing my lips against her ear. "Tell me you don't want me to, and I'll back off."

Reign catches her breath before saying, "I do... I do want you, Micah."

Our lips collide again in a steamy kiss. It lasts for the longest minute ever before I tear away and ease down to her stomach, pulling up her damp blouse so I can tease her stomach with my tongue.

Her light moans intensify my hardness. Oh man, I want her badly. I have to touch her, feel her, and taste her. I need every part of Reign.

I manage the strength to pull away again to hurry out of my sweats and unbutton her jeans, hauling them down to her ankles. I look at her face for any sign of hesitation before taking them off completely.

She braces up, combs her fingers through my hair, and pulls her blouse over her head, tossing it to the floor.

When she lies back down, Reign hugs her breasts—still concealed in her blue lace bra. I caress her thighs while making my way up to her satin panty, taking it off.

As I crawl back over her exceptionally curvy, sexy figure, she gasps when my hardness rubs against her. Gently, I move her hands away from her chest and reach under her back to unclasp her bra. She releases a shaky breath when I trail my fingers across her nipples.

"Micah," she whimpers.

I stop and regard her expression. She looks so nervous. The look you see on the face of a girl who's never done this before.

"I'm a virgin," she whispers, confirming it.

Honestly, I'd assumed she'd gone all the way with Nate already. He didn't seem like the 'let's wait' type. But now I'm unsure if we should go through with what we were obviously about to do only a few seconds ago.

Easing up, I look into her eyes and ask, "Do you want to stop?"

Reign places her hands on my back and pulls me back on her. "No," she murmurs, parting her thighs beneath me.

As nervous as she is, her yearning for me to satisfy her desire peppers her voice.

"Tell me what you want," I tease, kissing her neck.

She runs her fingers down my back as she whispers, "I want to feel you inside me."

I reach over to the table by my bed and take a condom out of the drawer. I ease off of her to slide it on and then gently position myself between her thighs. Her body quivers as I gradually enter.

Linking my fingers with hers, I move with care, mindful of Reign's reaction, ready to stop if it hurts too much and she wants me to. But when I glimpse the pleased look on her gorgeous face and see her eyes beam with anticipation, I know she wants this as much as I do.

TWENTY-SIX

Reign

HOLY SHIT! My first time is mind-blowing! There's no candlelight. No slow music or rose petals splattered across the sheets. It's only me, Micah, and the rain. That's enough. He's enough. It's perfect.

Once the icky sensation passes, my body bursts open with an immense amount of emotions. I relax beneath him, surrendering to the warmth between my thighs as Micah gently thrusts back and forth, groaning with pleasure.

"Oh..." I breathe, his grunts accompanying mine.

I travel up and down his strong, muscular back, pressing my fingers deeper into his skin. To my surprise, I'm braver than I expected, nibbling on his ear and neck. I tightly wrap my legs around his lower back and moan over and over, "Don't stop."

Micah makes love to me until we both explode from pleasure. Out of breath and drenched in sweat, he peels away from me because we can go no more.

He collapses on his back but clings to my hand as I settle my own thrashing heart. He struggles to ease over and kiss me tenderly on the lips before lying back on his side and placing an arm over me. We stare at each other for a long moment until he closes his eyes.

And to the calming sound of rain and Micah's now labored breathing, I shut my eyes and give in to sleep.

Waking up, I notice it's still dark and raining out. I don't have to look for my phone to see the time because I know it's late. My parents will be enraged when they notice I'm not in bed and my car is missing. But I don't want to think about that right now. I refuse to leave and disrupt the beautiful moment.

Micah's asleep next to me. He looks absolutely peaceful, with his hand swathed over me protectively. I feel it tighten when I shift a little. I move over and kiss him softly on the forehead. His eyes flutter open.

"Hmm... You've been admiring me, huh?" He nuzzles me closer and grins. "You can't get enough."

"You're right," I say before kissing his lips. "I can't."

We gaze at each other, drowning in adoration. Micah touches my cheek and runs his fingers up and down my arm, sending chills all over my naked body.

After another minute, I break the silence. "I want to know everything." There's still a great mystery about him that I want to unravel now that we've connected in such a way. "Tell me more about your grams and what your life was like in Haxtun."

His face turns tense, but he speaks anyway. "Grams meant the world to me. My whole life, I wanted to make her happy and be the best I could...." He trails off as a sad memory crosses his mind. "Guess I failed her."

I crumple my forehead, wondering how this amazing guy could fail anyone. "What do you mean?"

Micah glances at the window as blue lights consume the room in a quick flash. A terrifying rumble follows. Startled, I snuggle closer to him.

He laughs at me. "Ooh, someone's afraid of a little thunder, huh?"

"Whatever."

As it quiets down again, I continue to question him. "What happened to your parents? You never told me."

He sucks in a razor-sharp breath before he says, "Reign, I might not have a shitload of problems like some, but there are things about me that I'm scared to tell you. My life isn't pretty. It's far from it."

I ease up and say, "Micah, I don't want pretty. I want honesty."

Pushing up, he relaxes his back against the headboard. I join him, holding his hand to let him know I'll never judge him.

"It's okay," I whisper. "You can tell me anything."

Micah peers into my eyes. His Adam's apple bobs as he gulps hard before saying, "Well, for one, my parents weren't together. I'm the product of a drunken one-night stand gone wrong. My mother left me with my dad and grams after I was born. I grew up without her."

I rub his arm. "She missed out."

He shakes his head and continues. "My dad never gave up drinking, and for most of my life, he was in and out of rehab. Eventually, he gave up and disappeared too."

"I'm sorry," I mutter lowly, kissing him on the cheek.

"Don't be. I never lacked anything growing up. My grandmother was incredible. If anything, I was spoiled." He forces a grin.

I can't imagine what my life would be like without my parents. I'm so grateful for them. But my heart breaks for Micah. From the array of emotions in his eyes, I discern the hurt caused by his parents and the loss of the only family he had.

Stroking his face, I assure him, "You have me now."

This time, his mouth turns up into the natural, sexy grin that I like. "You're so sweet."

"Am I?" I tease, kissing his forehead and nose before making my way to his lips. He tightens his grip on me as he deepens the kiss.

It feels as if he fears he'll lose me, too, and almost as if there's still something he's holding back.

I pull away to meet his gaze. "Anything else you want to share?"

That dark shadow covers his face again, and Micah breaks away from my eyes.

"I was in—" he starts.

My phone buzzes on the floor, providing an interruption so he doesn't have to say another word.

"It's probably my mom," I sigh, looking at him with a sad expression.

"Answer it," he says.

"But I don't want to leave."

Micah lifts his hands and cups my face. Then he places my damp strands behind my ears. "We have many more nights like this to come. I'm sure of it." But his eyes say otherwise. He doesn't look so sure.

Nodding, I slide down to the edge of the bed and reach for my phone, still inside the pocket of my wet jeans. I look at the screen and see two missed calls. Both are from Mom.

"I checked with Mrs. Norman," she bombards me the instant she answers when I call her back. "She said that Claudia's fast asleep and you're not there. Not to mention, your car isn't parked outside."

"Mom, I can explain—"

"I'm sure you can as soon as you get back in this house."

I let out a deep sigh once I'm off the phone. Micah comes up to my back and nestles me in his strong and very naked body.

"I have to go," I tell him.

He turns me to face him. "So it seems."

Getting up from the bed, I put on one of his t-shirts and sweatpants. I'm in for it, going home in a guy's clothes, but there's no way I'm putting back on my drenched attire.

Eyeing me from head to toe, he grins widely. "Cute. Big trouble, but cute."

I shrug. "Pray for me."

Micah walks me downstairs to the main door. He kisses me again and squeezes me tightly in his arms. I pull out of his grasp to open the door and leave, but before I can run to my car, he touches my hand and says, "Thank you."

I peer back, smiling as I ask, "For what?"

He kisses me one more time. "For choosing me."

Mom and Dad greet me with appalled looks as I enter the living room. Their eyes seem to widen more after seeing Micah's t-shirt and sweatpants.

"I'm not even going to ask about your..." Mom gestures with her hand before saying, "clothes. But I did tell you not to go out, and you snuck out of the house, anyway."

"When did you even start sneaking out?" Dad adds, rubbing his forehead.

I'm still so mesmerized by Micah and him being all over me tonight that I can't come up with a sensible excuse.

"Reign?" Dad prods, growing impatient. "It's almost three a.m. Where were you?"

I shake my head and mumble, "Just... out."

Amazed by my answer, they look at each other and then back at me.

"Were you drinking?" Mom asks, accusation cutting through her voice.

"No, I don't drink." That much is true.

"You used to not do a lot of things," Dad mutters, "Sneaking out being one of them."

They both look so tired. So old these days.

"It's late," Mom finally says, massaging her temples. "We'll talk about this later. Go to bed."

Obediently, I leave them in the living room and saunter upstairs, taking my time to slip out of Micah's clothes—sure to inhale his intoxicating scent before I crawl into bed.

Thoughts of him swarm my head while I lie there in the dark, staring at the ceiling. I can't stop thinking about the way his strong hands felt against my skin, his fresh, out-of-the-shower scent devouring me, and more than anything, the passionate way in which he made love to me.

Gawd! Losing my virginity turned out to be way better than I expected. It's a night I will never forget, and I only want to be with Micah so much more now.

I think of him for another few minutes before my brain becomes tired, and I fall right to sleep.

I feel the warmth of the sun prick my face, and I open my eyes. It's no longer raining. Birds chirp outside, and it sounds like someone's playing reggae music downstairs. We haven't played music in the house in so long.

Pushing off the covers, I sit on the side of the bed and stretch my hands over my head. I'm feeling tired because I barely slept. I reach for my phone, seeing it's almost ten o'clock. Shit! I'm late for work.

I rush to the bathroom to shower fast, all the while wondering why Mom didn't wake me. After showering, I slip into a green summer dress and brown sandals and scamper downstairs, still yawning.

It's surprising to see Dad at the stove, making his special hash browns and egg white nests, while Mom's taking water bottles out of the refrigerator and packing them inside a cooler.

They're both wearing casual clothes, with Mom in an orange maxi dress and her lightly colored blonde hair pulled back loosely into a bun, while Dad's in dark blue shorts and a Hawaii-looking tropical shirt.

"What's going on?" I ask, standing in the doorway of the kitchen.

They look over in sync. Mom shuts the fridge door and walks to the island, gesturing for me to come and sit at the table as she brings over three plates.

"It's the fourth of July, so I figure I'd close the restaurant today, and we'll have a barbecue. Nice dress, by the way," she says, spinning to go back to the kitchen counter.

"Thanks," I reply. "But why are you closing? You never close, not even on holidays."

She walks back to the table with two platters. "There's always a festival in the square, and we don't get many customers on days like today, either." She sets them in the middle of the table. One has Dad's hash brown egg white nests, and the other has her maple pancake muffins. We always have those on July Fourth, but we haven't in a long time.

"Does this have anything to do with you selling the restaurant? Are you slowly starting to close it?"

"Honey, let's not talk about that," Mom says, sitting at the table. Dad joins us shortly.

Changing the subject so I don't kill their happy mood, I inquire about the barbecue instead. "Is it just us, or did you invite friends?"

"Well, a few of our friends are coming, and of course, Claudia and Mrs. Norman," Dad answers. "I also invited—"

"Can Micah come over?" I blurt out.

They glance at me with widened eyes. "Of course," Mom replies. "But why only him? I'm inviting everyone from the restaurant, anyway."

"Oh." I smile awkwardly.

Dad studies me with suspicion as he eats his muffin. Swallowing what's in his mouth, he says, "We still need to talk about last night."

"Yes, but later," Mom tells him, sensing the awkward vibe.

I lower my head to my plate and cut into one of his egg-white nests, not saying another word.

After breakfast, I help Dad set up chairs on the deck. The whole time, I notice his forehead wrinkling, and he keeps flashing me curious stares like he wants to talk to me about something, but not sure how to begin.

I bring out paper plates and plastic utensils while he sets up his tiki bar. He finally comes out and says something before I walk back into the kitchen. "You know, your mom and I never really talked to you about..." He pauses and scratches his head, searching for words. Oh gosh, my dad's trying to talk to me about sex. Like seriously? I'm almost nineteen. Isn't this conversation a little too late?

"It's just..." he rambles. "We want you to know we love you and... you're a special girl... Guys should appreciate you, respect you... Well, you know?"

I nod at every word and stifle my laughter. "I understand, Dad."

"Hello," Mrs. Norman calls, coming out of the kitchen with Claudia on her heels. I feel so relieved. They're saving me from the uncomfortable situation.

"Happy Fourth, Aldridge!" Claudia squeals. She sashays up to me in her sleeveless yellow maxi dress, blowing on a red star clacker.

"Oh, geez," Dad fans her off and walks over to the grill. He busies himself with it while Mrs. Norman helps prepare refreshments.

Claudia tows me to my room, wanting to know everything that happened last night. "So, did you guys do it?" she asks the second I shut the door.

"Talk about no filter," I scoff, plopping onto my bed.

She sinks beside me and bumps my arm. "You two sure move fast. I guess you had a lot of sexual tension from the start, so it makes sense you couldn't wait any longer."

I giggle shyly. "Who said we did anything?"

"Puh-lease," she snorts. "Mrs. Norman told me your mom was looking for you last night. I figure you were at his house, and there's no way you can convince me that you guys didn't hook up. So, how was your first time?"

"Is it slutty?" I ask. "I'd just broken up with Nate."

She jolts up on her elbows. "Of course not."

I ease up and sit cross-legged in the middle of the bed. "It was amazing, Claudia. Being with Micah is..." I smile to myself. "It's just... beautiful."

"Aww, how adorable." She lies flat on her back and plays with my pillow. "Will you tell your parents you're seeing him now?"

"Maybe I should wait."

She narrows her eyes. "Why?"

"Well, I still need to tell them I broke up with Nate, and I'm not sure how Mom will feel about me and Micah seeing each other."

"Pfft." She nudges my arm. "You're always so worried about what your parents think. Honestly, I cannot wait until we go to Miami. I'm definitely going to get you to loosen up."

The trip! I haven't told Micah about it.

"So, any plans for your nineteenth bday?" she asks.

"Nothing major. A party with you and my parents and Micah." I giggle at his name, making Claudia laugh at me.

We hang out in my room for a while until I hear the door and Mom's boisterous laugh as she greets her friends. Then she bellows for us to come downstairs.

Reaching the bottom step behind Claudia, I see Micah and John strolling in behind the Richards. Micah looks simple in a white shirt, washed-out jeans, and sneakers, yet there's something so sexy about him. It's as if I'm seeing him in a new light.

His gorgeous sea-blue eyes find mine, and my heart starts to sprint. A sly grin spreads across his lips, igniting the fire between my legs. I want to feel him inside me again, to sprawl me across his sheets and have his way with me.

My naughty thoughts take over, and everything disappears. All that's left is Micah and me.

Claudia elbows me, and I snap out of the spell to say hello to Mr. and Mrs. Richards. I laugh like an idiot when I shake their hands.

Before I can utter a word to Micah, Mom leads everyone through the kitchen and out to the deck, where Dad is grilling hotdogs and burgers.

I feel as if I'm on the grill, too. The heat's rushing all over me. Damn, this guy has invoked something intense and untamable within me. I have no idea how I'll make it through the day without running my hands all over his body.

It's going to be one long, scorching day.

TWENTY-SEVEN

Micah

I FIND IT interesting how I make Reign so nervous by only staring at her. The glimmer in those sensational eyes tells me she's remembering last night. With any luck, we'll find a way to at least brush lips before the day ends.

John's talking about something. I can't hear a word. My attention stays fixed on Reign across from me. Her mom's friends are questioning her about college and her business major. She keeps her gaze steady on me as she speaks. I can't help but lower my eyes to her soft lips, wanting to taste them again.

"Excuse me, Micah." Mrs. Aldridge's voice draws me away from Reign. I wonder if she noticed me gawking at her daughter with a dirty smirk on my face.

When I turn, I realize she's towing her husband over to me. So that's where Reign inherited her cinnamon-brown hair and hazel eyes. She resembles him a lot.

John, Claudia, and Aislin resume their conversation as I break away from them. My stomach clenches because, holy shit, I'm meeting Reign's father.

"Micah, this is Ben, my husband. Ben, this is Micah, the new employee I was telling you about."

She told him about me? Should I be worried?

I straighten and reach for his hand. Mr. Aldridge grips mine firmly as he regards me in the same intense way Reign likes to read people.

"Pleasure to meet you, sir," I say politely.

He nods. "Likewise. Sophia says you're a great employee."

I can't help but smile modestly. "Thank you, Mrs. Aldridge. I do my best."

The doorbell rings, and she slips away, hastening her steps to the kitchen. I feel I'm about to break out in sweat from the way Mr. Aldridge is staring at me. It's as if he knows something.

Please, God. Please don't let him know about juvie.

He motions over my shoulder and says, "You and Reign must have gotten close. She was asking if we invited you specifically."

Ahh! So that's what this is about. He suspects us.

"We've become good friends," I say. I'm not sure how he'd feel if he knew just how close. "You have a great daughter. She has a big heart."

Mr. Aldridge bobs his head and drinks his cocktail, watching me over the glass. He shakes it afterward and hums. "I don't think I mixed this right. I'll make another. Would you like one, son?" The term throws me a tad, and I actually think of my father.

"Micah?"

"Hmm... Oh." I quickly straighten and answer, "Yes, sir. Thank you."

I stand in place and catch my breath as Mr. Aldridge wanders over to his tiki bar, making us two glasses of whatever he's drinking.

A gentle hand touches my back. I nearly jump out of my skin when Reign whispers fast, "Wait a few minutes after I go inside, then come upstairs."

She struts off as Mr. Aldridge turns and starts back my way. He didn't see her talking to me. Thank God.

He hands me a glass as he reaches me.

"Thank you," I say.

"Obviously, it's non-alcoholic," he chuckles.

We drink at the same time.

"So, uh, you're nineteen, Sophia says..." He waits for me to confirm.

"Yes, sir," I reply, my palms turning sweaty. "I'll be twenty this October."

"Call me Ben. Any plans for college?"

I calm my nerves to answer, "Not yet, sir. Still looking at my options."

"Hm."

Maybe I should have lied. He seems displeased with my answer. I didn't know I'd face an interrogation today. My impression prior to being invited by her Mom was that Reign hadn't said anything to her parents about us.

Mr. Aldridge flashes a half-smile before slanting to move away. "Well, enjoy yourself, Micah. I'll relieve Paul at the grill."

"Thank you, sir."

Thank the heavens.

I watch him walk over to the grill, and then I turn my eyes toward the kitchen door. I want to go inside and meet Reign upstairs, but I'm scared that Mr. Aldridge or even Mrs. Aldridge will see me.

I look around the deck for my boss. She's busy entertaining her friends. Mr. Aldridge seems caught up in a conversation about baseball with Mr. Richards. Claudia's dancing with John to a Bob Marley song blasting from the speaker. Aislin is glaring at them a few feet away.

Everyone seems preoccupied.

This is my chance.

Taking a deep breath, I discreetly make my way from the deck and into the kitchen, placing my drink on top of the island as I hurry into the entrance and sneak upstairs. I have no idea which room belongs to Reign.

As I'm about to whisper her name, a door on the right cracks open, and she sticks her head out. Teasingly, she points her index and calls me over.

I bustle to the door, slipping inside. The moment she closes it, my lips find hers. I draw her into my arms and run my hands all over her body.

Reign moans and runs her tongue against my bottom lip. Then she starts kissing my neck. She lifts my shirt and touches my stomach, making her way up to my chest. In a whisper, she asks, "You think we can?"

I pull away to look at her. "Think we can what?"

She smiles, kisses me lightly on the lips, and places her back against the door. She hoists up her dress and pulls down her black panties, tossing it at me.

Breathing hard, she trails her eyes over me—hungry and waiting for me to take her.

"Are you okay, though?" I look down at her bottom half. "Last night was your first time."

A flirty grin parts her lips. "I'm fine." She kisses me tenderly.

I glance behind at the window. It's open, and I can hear laughter coming from outside. At any moment, someone will notice that we're both missing. Hopefully, it won't be her parents.

Looking at Reign, I say, "Maybe we shouldn't. It's risky, and I don't want your dad to kill me. I think he suspects there's something between us."

She shakes her head and whispers, "We'll be quick. Please, Micah. I've wanted you the moment you stepped through my front door." She plants kisses all over my face and neck, trails her fingers down below my waist, and caresses me there.

"Shit! You're making me so hard."

Reign wraps her arms around me, locking me against her body. That's all it takes for me to forget about being caught.

I pull down the zipper, unbutton my jeans, and drop it to my ankles. She tugs at the waist of my boxers, then yanks it down, revealing my hardness. I pick up her left leg, move her dress out of the way, and ease into her.

She gasps and tightens her hold on me, digging into my upper back. As I lift her other leg, Reign locks them around me. Her heart accelerates against mine. Air gushes from her as I drive up and down, making her squirm and cling to me even more.

Her body shivers. Nails dig into my shoulders. She purrs and exhales in sheer pleasure. I almost relieve myself inside of her but think better of it. As much as I don't want to, I ease out of her and back away. Pulling up my jeans, I get myself together and take a moment to cool down.

"You're trouble," I tell her.

She laughs and winks at me. "It's your fault. You've corrupted me."

Reign steadies her breathing, fixes her dress, and hurries into the bathroom. She returns shortly and puts on her underwear, smiling brazenly with me.

"You know we could get caught, right?" I remark, keeping an eye out the window.

"I'm sorry," she giggles. "I wanted to be with you so bad, Micah. I don't know what it is. You make me feel..."

I flick back to her. She's staring at me, speechless. Her eyes are like a whole different world, inviting me in. I fill the distance and cradle her face, kissing her softly.

When I manage to wrench myself away, I tell her, "You make me feel like that, too. You're so beautiful."

She rolls her eyes and laughs short. "You're not so bad yourself."

"I know. I'm super hot, and you can't get enough of me."

"Ha." She laughs and pushes me back playfully. "How presumptuous."

I run a hand through my hair and pose like a model for her. "I'm only stating the obvious."

Turning sideways, she contains her laugh and says, "Okay, Mr. Superhot, let's go downstairs before they notice we're missing."

Reign heads out first, with me following slowly behind. When she reaches downstairs and walks into the kitchen, I hear her mom before I turn the corner. I stay back on the stairs so she doesn't see me.

"There you are. Nate's here with his parents."

My chest tightens.

"Why are they here?" Reign asks. "Did you invite them?"

"I did," Mrs. Aldridge answers, sounding surprised. "Why do you look so upset? Did you two fight? I thought that's who you were with last—"

"I wasn't with Nate last night," Reign admits in an innocent tone. "Look, Mom, there's something I have to tell you."

Silence engulfs the room until a familiar voice breaks in, turning my stomach. I clench my fist and try to fight back my anger.

"Hey, babe. My parents have an early birthday gift for you since they won't be here to help you celebrate."

Babe? An early birthday gift? When *is* Reign's birthday? I feel horrible that I still don't know those little things. Then again, I haven't been completely honest either.

She starts to say, "Nate, you—"

"Come say hi," he cuts her off. "They miss you."

I'm waiting for Reign to tell him to leave, clue in her mom about their breakup, and that this guy is clearly a lunatic. But it doesn't happen. She's not saying anything. She doesn't even mention me.

I hear footsteps leading out of the kitchen. As I peer around the doorway, I see them on the deck with a couple gushing over Reign, giving her a large gift. I can't believe the fake smile on her face as she accepts it, hugs them back, and pretends like we didn't just have sex in her bedroom. To make it worse, that moron places his arm around her shoulders like they're still together. Are they? Did she lie to me?

Striding over to the island, I pick up my drink and chug the rest. I'm boiling over with anger and should probably get the hell out of here. But I can't. I like her a lot. And I'm not losing another person I care about.

I walk out to the deck. Reign glances at me, seeming remorseful. The smirk on Nate's face falters when he sees me. He looks at Reign, then back at me. *Yeah, that's right. I stole your girl.*

Stepping away from his parents, he moseys up to me, asking, "What are *you* doing here, bum?"

I laugh short and straighten in his face. "Her mom invited me, prick." I fight the urge to sock him, walking to the tiki bar for another drink instead.

Aislin saunters up to me. She keeps her voice low as she advises, "Dude, I hope that's not alcohol. That definitely won't look good to the company we're in."

"I'm not having alcohol," I retort, waving my punch in her face.

She blows out an air of relief. "Cool. I just thought that idiot had snuck under your skin."

Pulling out a chair, she sits down and pats the stool next to her. I sit with my back turned to the bar, watching Reign with Nate's parents.

I'm waiting for the ball to drop, for her to tell them and everyone else the truth. That it's me she's with now. Why won't she do it already, so it'll be my arm around her waist, laughing with her parents?

"I'm not good enough for her," I hear myself say.

"What?" Aislin remarks, touching my shoulder. "What do you mean?"

I glance at her and confess, "Reign broke up with Nate to be with me."

Her face brightens before she nods in her understanding. "Don't get upset. She probably doesn't want to ruin the day for her parents. Look how happy they are." She adds as I peer over at them, "I don't think Mrs. Aldridge has smiled this much in weeks. I think this is her last summer as the owner of *Captain's Choice*. Something's up, and she's probably waiting for the right time to tell us."

I'm amazed by the sadness that masks her face. It's the first time I've seen Aislin wear her emotions so visibly.

I follow her gaze and notice she's watching John. He's having an entertaining conversation with Claudia. They can't stop making each other laugh.

"You should tell him," I say to her.

Aislin drinks before she replies, "What are you on about?"

"John. It's obvious."

She glances across the deck at him, frowns, then carries her gaze back to her drink.

I look at Reign, happy that at least now she's keeping her distance from Nate and avoiding his parents, too, chatting with Mrs. Richards instead.

As the day winds down, Nate's parents finally leave, and others start to head out as well. Reign looks at me.

I want to be mad at her, but I can't. Aislin's words repeat in my head, and I feel as if I should let Reign handle it her way. No matter how badly I want to shout to the world that she's mine. Despite what I've done in the past, I have something great in my life.

TWENTY-EIGHT

Reign

MAYBE I AM a bad girl. I had sex with Micah in my room, and shortly after, I pretended to be dating Nate still so as not to embarrass Mom for inviting him and his parents to our barbecue.

But what about Micah? I must have hurt him.

I've watched him the past few hours, sitting with Aislin at Dad's tiki bar. Jealousy pricks at my heart as I wonder what they're talking about.

She managed to make him laugh earlier. No matter how short and halfhearted it was, it still bothered me. I don't want him talking to other girls, not even my friends. Then again, he probably hates me for not telling everyone about us.

Claudia throws her arms around my shoulder and jerks me lightly. "Whatcha thinking about, girlie?"

I fake a smile as I answer, "Nothing."

"Anyway, my dad and step-monster will be back from their vacation tomorrow. Think your mom will let me hang out at the restaurant since it's Sunday?"

"I guess."

"Well," She untangles her arms, "I'm going to meet someone real quick and be back here in time for your dad's fireworks. Everyone knows he puts on the best show."

"Okay." I nod and watch as she strolls off. I don't ask who she's meeting because it doesn't matter to me now. I'm only interested in making sure Micah isn't mad at me.

Dad's cleaning the grill, and Mrs. Norman and John are helping Mom bring stuff inside, so I catch my breath and walk over to Micah and Aislin at the bar.

Wrapped up in a conversation, they don't notice me until I say, "Hey."

When Micah turns and looks at me, my legs feel weak, and my heart thumps faster.

"Look who finally remembered me," he says. He doesn't sound like his usual playful self. "What's up?"

"I'm sorry. I didn't have a chance to tell them earlier, and they'd already invited Nate and his parents."

He doesn't say anything, only stares at me. Aislin slides off the stool and takes up her drink. "I'll help your mom clean up before the fireworks."

When she walks away, I ask him, "What were you two talking about?"

Micah raises a brow and stands. "Are you jealous?"

A part of me wonders if he was deliberately giving Aislin his full attention to bug me.

"No," I lie. "Just that, you two seemed to have exchanged a lot more words than you usually do at the restaurant."

He releases a sarcastic laugh before saying, "At least she acknowledges me."

That only makes me feel guiltier. I lower my eyes to the concrete to evade his piercing gaze.

"Enjoy the fireworks," he says under his breath. "I'm heading out."

When I look up, Micah grabs his cup and brushes my arm lightly as he steps past me. I watch as he makes his way inside the kitchen.

No. I don't want him to leave like this.

I hurry over to the kitchen, seeing him head for the front door.

"Micah," I call out. His hand freezes on the door handle, and he looks back at me. So does everyone else, including my confused parents.

"Um..." I swallow and come out with it. "Micah and I are dating now."

John laughs because someone like him probably thinks my announcement is dramatic. Aislin slaps him on the arm to be quiet. Mrs. Norman smiles warmly at me. Dad's face is unreadable, and Mom looks worried.

"Well, can't say I didn't notice," Dad remarks. He glances behind at Micah, still standing at the door.

Finally, he blows a short breath and walks back into the kitchen.

"Why didn't you say something?" Mom asks, moving closer to me.

"I didn't want you to feel bad about inviting Nate and his parents, and you guys looked so happy today. I didn't want to ruin it."

"Oh, honey." She rubs my arm.

"You broke up with Nate for Micah?" Dad clarifies.

"Yes and no." I gnaw at my bottom lip.

"Yes and no?" Mom repeats.

"I've been trying to make it work with Nate, but our relationship didn't feel right. When Micah came along..." I look at him, skin tingling as he smiles halfway. "We started spending time together, and I developed feelings for him that I'd never felt for anyone before. I'm happier with him. I laugh more. I feel so relaxed and... safe." Walking over to Micah, I place my arm around his back. "He's the guy I want to be with. Not Nate."

"But you two barely know each other," Dad retorts.

I shrug. "I know enough."

"Micah," Mom cuts in. "I thought you were leaving Newport after this summer?"

"No, ma'am." He holds my hand, adding softly, "I have a reason to stay."

"Okay. But what about that... thing... Did you—" She stops herself from finishing.

Confused, I refocus on Micah. His eyes are pleading as he gazes at her. And there's a combination of worry and fear engraved on his face.

"What, Mom?" I prod, steering back to her.

She waves me off. "Nothing."

Silence engulfs the kitchen until Dad breaks in, "Fireworks. Let's get the show on the road."

Everyone files out, leaving Micah and me with Dad back in the kitchen. He hums and says, "Just don't move too fast."

"We won't," I tell him. He might have a break down if he knew just how much our relationship has progressed in the last forty-eight hours. But that's probably why he gave me that jumbled lecture on sex earlier.

Dad turns to go outside but lingers by the kitchen door, looking sideways at us. "I have to say that I've noticed a change in you, honey." Eyeing Micah, he adds, "Don't make her cry, or you'll have me to deal with."

"Yes—I mean, no sir. I won't."

I stifle my laugh; it's funny seeing Micah so flabbergasted and afraid of my dad, who's like a big teddy bear to me.

He finally steps outside, leaving us alone. Micah kisses me softly before we join everyone on the sand, watching with excitement as Dad fills the evening sky with a blast of dazzling red, white, and blue displays.

He continues the spectacle as night falls, and Claudia comes back in time for the grand finale. She looks happier than ever. I make a mental note to ask her about it later.

I snuggle up to Micah on a blanket in the sand. He makes me feel content. I don't hear Mary's cries in the ocean or see her face. And for the first time in a long while, I don't feel as guilty for her death.

TWENTY-NINE

Micah

I'VE COME ACROSS people with a fear of the ocean, but this isn't the same thing. What's holding Reign back isn't a phobia. It's deeper. She's inside a mental prison where she sees her sister drowning and can't do anything to save her. For Reign, stepping foot into the ocean is like facing Mary, and she's still afraid of that.

We've been at it since the day after the Fourth of July when she believed she could handle it. Now, almost two weeks later, I still can't get Reign to step any further than the shore. Each time she attempts, she'll turn and hurry back up the sand when the water touches her feet.

"I thought you said she was gone? What was that talk about the weekend at your house?" I ask her.

She brings her knees up to her chest and slumps over them. "I don't know, a momentary calm."

I reach my hand down to her. "Let's try again. This time, I'll hold your hand the entire time."

Reign shakes her head. "It's useless. I've already tried with Claudia. It doesn't matter if I'm starting to forgive myself. I'll always see my sister's face."

"What does she look like?" I ask, sitting beside her.

She spins her head and blinks in her confusion. "What do you mean?"

"The expression on Mary's face," I explain. "Is she angry? Scared? Is she screaming at you?"

"She's not doing anything, at least, not anymore. Not since *you*. These days, she looks at me like she's waiting."

"Then go to her," I say. "She wants you to let it go completely, not just the blame but the sadness over her death and whatever else is eating at you."

A smile sneaks its way to her lips. "Gosh, how are you not calling me crazy right now? How are you still with me knowing all this?"

I lean over and brush her face. Her body quivers. "That's because I get you."

She kisses me before I get the chance, pushing me down into the sand to straddle me.

"Whoa, look who's getting kinky in public." I laugh and bring my hands down to her butt, cupping them.

She wiggles out of my grasp and hops up, dusting sand off her shorts and arms.

I spring to my feet and ask, "Wanna try again?"

A slight frown appears as she glances out at sea. After a beat, she looks at me. "No, let's head back. It's almost time for work."

Staring down my nose at her, I raise an eyebrow. "I meant to toss me to the ground and straddle me one more time." Licking my lips, I eye her from head to toe and add in a deeper, flirtier voice, "Mmm. I don't mind a good wrestle in the sand."

Reign scoffs and folds her arms. "Is that so? Now, who's kinky?"

"Hey, you know me? I like excitement."

"So it seems."

Laughing, she rolls her eyes and nudges over her shoulder. "Let's get out of here."

I drape my arm around her waist as we head for her car.

"So, I'm having a dinner for my birthday. It'll only be my parents, Claudia, Mrs. Norman, and the guys from the restaurant. You're coming too, right?"

"Of course, I wouldn't miss it for the world," I tell her. "What would you like? I'm terrible at buying gifts."

She pouts and wobbles her head. Her ponytail dances in her back. "Uh-huh, you have to surprise me. I'm sure whatever you get, I'll appreciate."

"Right," I exhale. "Girls always say that, then complain when guys buy them crap. I won't risk it. I'll bring Claudia with me. She'll know what to get you."

When we reach her car, my cell phone rings. I glimpse the screen. It's Greg. I haven't told him my decision yet.

"What's wrong?" she asks, noticing my delay.

I tuck my phone back into my pocket and slide onto the passenger seat, closing the door. She hops in and shuts her door, waiting for me to tell her what's wrong.

My phone starts to vibrate again, but I ignore it. That only intensifies her curiosity.

"Who's calling you?" She wrinkles her forehead. "I'm surprised. I never hear your phone ring."

Looking at her, I lift a shaky hand and stroke her cheek. I've never been so scared of losing someone. But she deserves to know. She's been nothing but honest with me, so I owe her the same.

"That was Greg. I probably have to go back to Haxtun soon."

Her eyes widen, and she sputters, "Who's Greg? Why do you have to go back? I thought you were staying in Newport?"

"It's not like I won't come back," I try to calm her. "I just have to take care of something."

"What?" She has this desperate expression on her face. She wants me to tell her everything.

I drop my hand from her face as I mentally scold myself for hiding it all this time.

"Who's Greg, Micah?" she urges me.

It's now. Damn it. I should tell her now. "I was in juvie for eight months."

Reign stares at me open-mouthed. "Oh... okay. Why were you there?"

The fearful look in her eyes scares me. She's piecing things together, trying to decipher what I could have done.

My heart races, and my palms begin to sweat as I relive that night in my head so that I can tell her everything.

"First off, my real name's Mitchel Stephens. Micah's my grandfather's name. Grams used to call me little Micah when I was growing up because I looked so much like him. Delaney is her maiden name."

She slumps forward and releases a razor-sharp breath. "You lied? I don't understand. Why did you—"

"Because I wanted a new start, and I didn't want anyone finding out about what Mitchel Stephens did in Haxtun. I didn't want it following me everywhere."

She flares her hands, asking in a biting tone, "What *did* you do in Haxtun?"

"I guess the only thing to hope for now is that you won't be mad at me. Though, you're already mad about me lying."

She turns her head slowly and cuts her eyes off me, looking at her fingers. "Just tell me the truth," she whispers.

After a brief pause, I begin, "It was exactly a month after my seventeenth birthday. That was the day my dad had taken off for good. It left me pissed at the world. I wouldn't even talk to Grams. Jason came by the house that evening and said there was a party out of town."

"Who's Jason?" she asks, bringing her eyes back to meet mine.

I collapse my head against the headrest and stare out the windshield at the ocean. "A friend I had. He wanted me to snap out of it, so I decided to go to the party. We were drinking, having a good time... I was trying to forget about everything. We left the party with Jason wasted. I didn't drink as much as he did, but I was still emotionally out of it.

"We were driving back to town in his truck, and then all of a sudden, Jason wanted to stop at our high school. He grabbed his bat from behind his seat; he had a bottle of vodka, and he wouldn't let me take it. We jumped the fence to the football field and snuck into the gym. I was following along because... I didn't know what he was going to do, and I didn't want to leave him alone..." I trail off for a moment.

"Because he's your friend," Reign says.

"*Was*," I correct, carrying my gaze to her. "He *was* my friend."

She urges me to go on. "So what happened?"

"Jason went to where the lockers were and started hitting everything and laughing. He was going on about how he was better than the other players on the baseball team. When we reached the glass display shelf where all the trophies were, he started swinging the bat like crazy; the glass shattered. His hands even had splinters in them, and blood was all over. But he didn't even budge. He kept hitting the trophies, breaking a couple of them. I tried to stop him, but he'd push me off every time. Now and then, he'd stop to drink more and, of course, to laugh. He loved to laugh. Everything was always a joke to him. Then he'd start to swing his bat again.

"I kept trying to calm him down. It was useless. Everything was a mess. I knew we were in serious trouble, so the only thing left to do was get out of there. That's when Lewis Harrison showed up."

"Who's that?" she mutters.

"School security guard," I reply. "He lived close by, so I guess he heard the noise and decided to check it out himself. Lewis saw my face first, and then he said my name. The look he gave me... He was so disappointed because he knew Grams. Guess he never expected me to be involved in vandalism. Jason, on the other hand, already had a rap sheet of bad behavior."

I stop and clench my fist because it's always hard to talk about, much less remember what happened next.

"Keep going," she urges. "Tell me everything."

"I was angry because of the way he stared at me; it was the same look my dad gave me like I was nothing. Lewis pointed at me and said he'd call the cops, and both of us were going to jail. His belittling glare still had me livid, so I ran after him. I shoved him hard into the lockers."

Reign gasps and covers her mouth with one hand. I look away from her eyes so I can keep talking, even though my voice is cracking up.

"Lewis lost his balance and fell to the floor. He'd hurt his back. I wasn't thinking straight. I kicked him in the stomach."

"Oh no," she breathes. "Micah..."

"Three times," I mutter, looking at my clenched fists. "Jason rushed over to us. He saw Lewis on the floor, and he shouted for me to hit him again. I told him no. That we should get out of there. By then, I was snapping back to my senses.

"I turned to leave, and that's when Jason raised the bat. Before I could reach for it, he'd already brought it down on Lewis' head."

I stop talking as my throat starts to burn. I'm having a hard time holding back my tears. Clearing the tightness in my throat, I continue, "Jason panicked when he realized what he'd done. He yanked on my shirt to take off with him back to his truck. I pulled away, staying with Lewis instead.

"Blood ran from his head. Even though he was still breathing, he couldn't keep his eyes open, and he didn't move. I called the cops. Jason was already gone by the time they showed up. They saw the damage and Lewis' injuries and arrested me. I deserved it because I hit him first. I probably deserve the same sentence as Jason."

"You don't deserve the same punishment. You tried to stop him."

I flinch when Reign touches my arm. I didn't expect her to even want to breathe the same air, much less still want to comfort me. "Micah, you were drinking. You were upset about your dad—"

"That's no excuse for hitting Lewis," I tell her, choking back on tears. "Because of what? So I could show him how tough I was? That I didn't need anybody looking down on me? That I'm good enough—"

"You are good enough. And you didn't hit him with a baseball bat. Jason did. He ran, and you stayed."

I shake my head and move her hand. "It doesn't matter; everyone said I should have gotten the same sentence as Jason. He went to jail for putting Lewis in a coma. I spent eight months in juvie. God!"

I wipe my face with the palm of my hand. "Grams... She was so ashamed of me. You know, people in town made me feel like I was the biggest loser in Haxtun. When I went away, a bunch of them kept calling her house. They tormented her because of what happened. Told her I was a screw-up like my alcoholic dad. Her health worsened while I was in juvie for doing something stupid, and then she died alone, disappointed in me."

I can't fight it anymore. Tears start to stream down my face as I tell her the one thing that hurts me more than anything else. "I feel like I broke her heart so much, it killed her."

"No, Micah." Reign pulls me into her arms and hugs me tighter than she's ever held me before. "It's not your fault. We all make mistakes, and I know your grandmother loved you. It's like what you told me, that we have to learn to cope and move on. I'm sure she'd want you to let it go."

I ease out of her embrace. "That's just it. Lewis Harrison is out of his coma, and he wants to see me. But I feel like such a coward. I don't think I can face him. I don't think I can go back there, Reign."

She lingers a moment as if she's seriously considering her next words. Then she wipes my cheek and tells me, "You have to. You can apologize to him face-to-face for what happened."

Taking a deep breath, I stifle back the sobs and toughen up, only to ask her, "Can you come with me?"

"What?" She brushes her loose strand behind her ear. "You want me to go to Haxtun with you?"

I nod. "I don't think I can do this without you. You have no idea how much strength you give me, Reign."

"Micah—Mitchel—"

"Micah," I tell her, reaching for her hand. "Just call me Micah. We can go there for a weekend, that's all. I just... I really need you with me."

Reign slips her hand out from under mine. Her hazel eyes penetrate my face, a mixture of sympathy and anger dwelling in them.

I consider the fact that not only did I lie about my name, but I also kept a good chunk of myself from her when she shared something deep with me. How selfish of me to ask her to share my burden and come back to my hometown.

I start to tell her, "You don't—"

She cuts me off, "Let me think about it. I need to soak this all in."

"Okay," I say in a low tone. "Thank you... for not freaking out as much as I thought you would. I should have told you from the beginning when we started getting closer."

"You should have," she says. "Instead of allowing this to continue eating away at your heart, dumbass."

I can't help but smile, appreciative of the fact that I've met such a wonderful girl. Maybe I can find the strength to face what I'm running from after all.

THIRTY

Reign

"WOW." Claudia releases a surge of air as she sits down with her back turned to her antique-looking dresser, resting her chin on the back of the chair. "That's quite a story he told you. So his name isn't even Micah?" she confirms, her pitch increasing on his name.

I lean against the wall with my legs outstretched on her bed, picking at the pillowcase. After Micah's confession, we didn't even have breakfast before work, and I didn't talk to him at all while at the restaurant.

Throughout the day, I kept replaying what he told me and him asking me to return to Haxtun with him to face Lewis Harrison.

Arriving at home, I cross to Claudia's house and tell her everything the second I step into her room. It's approaching midnight now, and I still have no idea what to do.

"Why is it so hard to return to Haxtun with him?" she asks.

"I don't know. I feel like it's something he has to do alone," I explain to her when she lifts a brow. "Like how

I have to get over my guilt. I mean, even if you or Micah hold my hand and walk with me into the ocean, I'll still be afraid. I have to take that leap alone. It's something like that."

Straightening, Claudia puts her red hair up into a loose bun, then comes over to the bed to lie down. I flatten on my back, resting my head on the pillow next to her.

"Okay," she murmurs. "So he hid the fact that he was in juvie—"

"And he lied about his name," I remind her, my voice sharp.

"Yes, yes. But have you considered that if Micah goes back to Haxtun alone, he might not return to Newport?"

I raise my head and look at her. "Are you saying he'll be more inclined to make his peace and come back only if I go with him?"

Seeing I'm taking her words too seriously, Claudia touches my arm and says softly, "Ignore me. I'm only spewing fuckery again. What do I know?"

She giggles to calm me down. I collapse my head back on the pillow.

"By the way, does he know you're going to Florida with me right after your birthday?"

"Oh... I still need to tell him that."

"Well, if he's back in Newport by then, he could come with us. I don't mind." Again, it sounds like she thinks he'll be gone a long time. "Guess that depends on when he goes to Haxtun, too."

"Guess so," I mutter, not saying more on the topic.

Pulling the covers over us, Claudia rolls onto her side and turns off the lamp. "Let's get some sleep."

"Okay," I say in a near whisper. "Goodnight."

An hour passes, and I'm still awake, considering what Claudia said. As much as I'm mad at Micah for lying and keeping juvie a secret, I don't want to choose not to accompany him to Haxtun only for him to decide he's not coming back to Newport. To me.

I sneak out of Claudia's room before daybreak and hurry to my house to change for the morning run. When I drive to the beach, Micah isn't there. Maybe he thought I wouldn't show up, so he decided not to come.

Even though I've lost interest in running by myself since I started doing it with him, I'll use the opportunity to consider Haxtun more.

A part of me wants to go, and a part of me is saying no, let him do it alone.

I jog for twenty minutes, then head back to the beach, stopping in the sand to watch the sunrise on the horizon. I don't feel captivated when Micah's not here observing it with me. Gosh, I like having him around so much. I like his broad grin and the small, sexy dimple on his right cheek; his addictive scent, the way he kisses me, the way he touches me.

I really want him to touch me right now. To be inside me, telling me over and over how much he wants me.

Swiveling, I jog back to my car and jump in, taking off immediately. I feel as if my insides are on fire, tempting me to drive like a maniac and run red lights.

When I finally reach his house, I park and hurry from the car, running up to the third floor as fast as I can and then pound on his door.

I don't care. My senses are all over the place right now, and only one thing is clear: I need Micah.

There's a warm, moist sensation between my thighs pushing me to take care of it. So overpowered by lust that I'm on the verge of ripping off my clothes outside his door. The second I think I'm about to erupt, Micah finally opens the door. This is perfect. He's shirtless, only wearing shorts.

He flicks his eyes over my face once and quickly tugs me inside. He slams the door shut and backs me up against it.

"Micah," I breathe. He lifts my hands and hauls my top over my head.

Like an animal that hasn't eaten in days, he kisses me aggressively, pulls at the waist of my tights, and squeezes my butt as he presses into me.

"Micah," I groan again. There are three words on my lips, but something's holding me back. I can't tell him, not yet.

I entangle my tongue with his as he devours my mouth. Reaching around his back, I claw at his skin and pull him harder. Micah unsnaps my bra, tossing it to the floor. He strays from my lips, kisses my chin, and traces my jawline until he reaches my neck. I tremble as he sticks his hand inside my underwear, finding what desperately needs his affection.

"Mmm," he groans in delight as he realizes how much I want him. Then he gently inserts his middle finger and uses it to pleasure me.

"Micah," I moan once more as I lift my leg to give him more access. Sliding a hand down his torso, I slip it inside his shorts. A grin parts my lips when I feel how hard he is. He wants me just as bad.

As if having enough, Micah slides my tights and underwear down to my ankles. I kick them off. We don't make it to his bed. Desire takes over, and we slither to the hardwood floor.

"Oh..." I quiver as Micah eases his way in, making love to me slowly, ravenously, and with more passion than before.

THIRTY-ONE

Micah

"WHAT JUST HAPPENED?" I ask moments later while we're cuddling after eventually reaching my bed.

"I don't know," she tells me, sounding exhausted. "I was at the beach, and then I wanted to see you right away."

I laugh teasingly. "I could tell. Guess you're not too mad at me for lying about my name and keeping secrets, then?"

Reign snuggles up to me and kisses my jaw. "I'm still a little upset about it, but I like you too much to stay mad."

Lowering my head to her face, I kiss her lightly on the lips and stroke her hair. I can't get over the way she looked earlier, standing in my doorway, panting.

There was so much passion in her eyes when she stared at me. And the way she held my body when I made love to her, it's as if it was our last.

I can't help but ask, "Did you decide if you want to come with me?"

Her face tenses. She looks away from my gaze. "I... don't know."

"It's okay if you don't," I tell her so she doesn't feel guilty.

Relief covers her face as she glances at me. "You sure? You'll be okay going back alone?"

I nod. "Truthfully, I've never felt more scared about anything the way I'm afraid of seeing Lewis again. But it'll be fine. I need to get past this."

Reign tips her chin up and kisses me. We stare at each other for a while before I glimpse the clock on the table by my bed. "It's almost eight. You don't want to be late for work and put me on your mom's bad side, do you?"

She wobbles her head and eases out of my arms as I climb out of bed to put on my sweats. Walking over to the kitchenette, I make her coffee and toast—since she came straight here after running—while she hauls back on her workout clothes.

"So, did you call that guy back?" she asks, putting on her sneakers.

I lean against the counter. "Not yet. I'll call Greg in a little."

Sitting down at the table, Reign rests her elbows on top of the placemat, studying me as she asks, "Who is he, anyway?"

"He was my counselor in juvie. He helped me a lot, not only with what happened to Lewis but with stuff having to do with my parents."

"I see." She picks at the placemat, contemplating something. "Are you thinking about going this weekend then?"

I sit across from her at the table. "Yeah, I probably will. So, guess I'm going to have to tell your mom—"

"But you're coming back, right?" There's uncertainty in her hazel eyes, like she's afraid I won't. "I mean, you just have to ask her for the weekend off, that's all. And my birthday's next week. You'll be here for that, right?"

Leaning forward, I reach for her hands. "Of course, I'm coming back, babe. Relax," I assure her. "Why wouldn't I?"

She shrugs. "I don't know. Maybe you'll go home and realize how much you missed it and decide to stay."

"The only way I'd stay in Haxtun is if you're there," I tell her. "Don't worry about that."

The sweet smile I adore returns, and she braces over the table to kiss me.

"I forgot to mention something," she says, settling back on the seat.

"What?" I press, playfully narrowing my eyes.

"Claudia and I have been planning this trip to Miami for a while back. It's for two weeks; we leave at the end of the month. She says you can come if you want..."

"Huh. That sounds like a girls' trip."

She shakes her head. "It'll be fine, you can come with us. Claudia won't mind."

"Babe, you don't have to invite me along. You can go have fun with your best friend," I say. "But you gotta get in the water, though. It won't be fun if you don't."

Reign twists her mouth to one side, saying, "I'll keep trying. I'll do it before we leave for Florida. I will."

"You can do it. I believe in you."

I hear the toaster and hop up to fix her a plate. We have breakfast together before Reign heads home to get ready for work.

On my way out, I call Greg to let him know I've decided to meet with Lewis this weekend. I have to suck it up and handle my problem.

"That's great, Mitchel," he enthuses. "I'll let them know you'll be coming then. Can I ask what changed your mind?"

"It's the right thing to do," I reply. "I never got a chance to apologize, and I want to."

Greg pauses a moment before he says, "That's good. It's part of your journey to moving on."

"I know."

"Well, I'll let them know. See you soon."

When I arrive at the restaurant, that broker from before, Dean Carmichael, is inside talking to John. He appears sympathetic, while John has a crooked look on his face. He's not happy, and he wants nothing to do with Mr. Carmichael.

I park my bike next to a metal post and walk through the door. The air is thick. I feel as if I've missed the whole shebang.

Aislin and Reign stop talking and glance at me. Mr. Carmichael turns away from John, striding over to me.

"Hey, we haven't met officially. I'm Dean," he says, reaching his hand out to shake mine.

I reply simply with, "Micah."

"Well, Micah. Good to meet you. I hope we'll have a pleasant working relationship from here on."

John snorts at his back. Wrinkling a brow, I twist and regard Reign's face. She shrugs and looks down at her fingers, chipping at her nails. It's what she does when she's thinking hard or isn't sure what to do.

Looking back at Dean, I ask, "What do you mean?"

A smug grin spreads across his face as he answers, "I've purchased *Captain's Choice* from Sophia. My consultant and I will be working to come up with strategies that will improve the restaurant."

"Improve how?" Aislin fires from across the room. She slowly walks over to him and drops her hands on her hips.

Dean slants and eyes her from head to toe. "Well, I'm considering changing the name to revamp the place." He clears his throat and adds, "Among other things." That probably means he's planning on letting them go.

Her eyes expand. "You're changing the name? You can't do that."

"Miss," he chuckles, finding her reaction amusing, it seems, "I *own* the place now. Yes, I can."

The door swings open, and we all twist to see Mrs. Aldridge entering. She studies our faces and lets out a deep sigh before stopping by Dean.

"Why are you all moping? It's not the end of the world."

"But Mom," Reign starts. "You love this place. We love this place."

"And it'll still be here," Mrs. Aldridge says, walking over to her daughter. She squeezes her shoulder.

Looking at the rest of us, she says, "It'll remain *Captain's Choice* until August. I've agreed to let Dean do whatever he wants after that. Now, please, don't look so depressed. You'll still have your jobs."

"Right," Aislin mumbles.

Mrs. Aldridge makes to say something to her, but three customers enter the restaurant.

Suddenly, we all scatter. Reign and Aislin tend to the customers. Dean walks out to his car to use his phone, and John does what he does best, which is to watch TV while he fishes around the bar.

I mosey to Mrs. Aldridge's office. Even though it's a hard time for her, I have to tell her I'm going back to Haxtun this weekend.

She's flipping through papers when I enter. "I know this is a bad time, but I'm hoping for a few days off to return to my hometown."

"You're going home?" she remarks, peering up at me from the papers.

"I need to take care of something," I explain.

"Does this have anything to do with juvie?" she asks.

"Yes, ma'am," I reply in a low tone.

She nods slowly, understanding. "And did you tell Reign, not only that you've been there but what you've done?"

"I have."

Her face relaxes. She sits back in her chair and studies me. "Micah, if you don't mind me asking, what happened in Haxtun?"

I look down at my hands. "I don't... um... I don't think I—"

"You were more comfortable telling Reign," she concludes.

Swallowing, I peer up at her again. "I'm sorry. It's just hard."

"It's okay. I understand." She releases a gush of air before saying, "I'm glad you opened up to her. It's never good to keep something that hurts inside. And I don't know what you've done, but I'm happy she's trying to do the same."

Mrs. Aldridge smiles at me. It's warm, kind, and beyond genuine. It's the way I wish my mother would smile at me if I ever met her.

"Well, get back out there," she says.

Nodding, I stand and head for the door. Before stepping outside, I twist and look at her sideways, saying, "Mrs. Aldridge, I'm sorry you had to sell your restaurant."

Her smile slowly fades. She glances at the floor and mutters, "Don't be. I've wanted to make a change for a while now. I guess it's just time for me to move on, too."

After work, Reign drives home to park her car. I follow her on my bike. Then she hops on, and I ride out to the beach.

She snuggles up in my arms as we stargaze, relaxing to the tranquil sound of waves as they roll ashore. The salty sea breeze clashes with the fruity scent of her hair as it blows in the wind. I gently stroke her head.

Reign exhales deeply before saying, "I wish we could spend more time together. It'll be like this when I start college, too. You'll be working during the day, and I'll be in class. Plus, I'll be in South Kingstown throughout the week. We'll only see each other in the evenings and on weekends. I wish we had more hours."

"Yeah, right," I chuckle. "I'm sure you'd get sick of me if we were together twenty-four-seven."

Easing out of my arms, she looks at me intensely. The pale moon casts a dim spotlight on her face.

"I could never get sick of you," she whispers, leaning forward to kiss me. Her mouth is like a drug—a really sweet one that keeps me hooked. No rehab in the world could break my addiction. Her body is my heaven. Man, I think I've fallen hard for this girl.

Reign collapses into my chest at the end of the kiss. She muffles something like, "Please come back." I'm not sure. When I lift her chin and gesture for her to repeat it, she shakes her head and smiles at me. We return to watching the stars.

An hour or so trickles pass before we head from the beach, and I walk next to her with my bike instead of riding us back to her house.

Reign asks me all kinds of questions about my childhood, what I did in Georgetown, and if I have ever been in a serious relationship before.

"Why does that matter?" I ask, bumping her arm lightly.

A shy smile tugs at her lips as she brushes back her hair behind her ears. "Because I feel like... I mean... I consider this, between you and me..." She glances at me for an instant as she says, "Serious."

"And?" I urge her to go on, finding her impeccably cute as she expresses herself.

"*And* I want to know that you feel the same. That you don't have a problem with us being exclusive."

I can't help the broad grin that finds its way to my lips. "Reign, believe me when I say I'm all yours. I consider this between us," I gesture with my hand, "serious, too."

A satisfied look masks her face. "Good," she mutters, slipping her small, soft hand into mine.

"This doesn't have anything to do with me going back to Haxtun, does it?"

"I'm making sure you don't have some hot crush waiting for you," she says jokingly.

I snort and dip my head back. "I have several super hot crushes waiting for me in my hometown. I was a soccer star in my high school, baby. Girls go crazy when they see me."

She scoffs and knocks my arm lightly. "You better behave, or I might give Nate a call while you're away."

Stopping instantly, I widen my eyes as if appalled. "You better not."

With a mischievous grin, Reign keeps walking down the sidewalk, swinging her hips as she hums the rest of the way.

I laugh and hop on my bike, riding up to her. I kiss her cheek and slap her butt as I pass. She squeals and runs after me, her beautiful laughter filling the night.

Circling, I ride back to her. She slows down and looks at me in wonder, grinning from ear to ear. I've never seen a happier girl in the world. Pulling up to her, she hops on my bike, and I kiss her again, this time sweetly on her mouth. Then we take off for her house.

I can't deny it. I have fallen. I'm in love with Reign.

THIRTY-TWO

Reign

Someone shakes my arm. When I open my eyes, I see Mary standing over my bed. She gives me a sneaky grin as she places her finger on her lips and indicates for me to be quiet.

She slants and tiptoes from my room. I climb out of bed and quietly follow her downstairs into the dark kitchen.

"Come on," she whispers, opening the glass door to the deck. I stride behind her as she walks down the wooden steps onto the sand.

"What are you doing?" I ask as she stops and stares at the dark ocean.

"I'm going for a swim," she says, smiling defiantly at me.

I look at the ocean for a fraction of a second, wondering why she'd want to go into such rough waters at night. Then I bring my attention back to her, asking, "Now? It's not safe."

Rolling her eyes at me, Mary proceeds to take off her blue PJs, pulls out her scrunchie, and shakes out her long ash-brown hair. "Yes, now," she jeers before dashing off into the ocean in her underwear.

Mary dives under for a moment, then pushes her head back above water, laughing excitedly. "Come on, Reign," she waves me over. "The water's great!"

I glance back at the house. Dad isn't working late in the shop tonight. He and Mom are fast asleep. They never let us go swimming at night and would be mad if they knew we were out in the ocean at this hour.

"Reign!"

The insistence in her voice draws back my attention. I want to be fun for Mary. She'll get mad at me again. So I take a few steps forward, keeping my eyes fixed on her. I can hardly see her face in the darkness, only the outline of her head and shoulders against the pale moonlight.

Mary dives under again, and this time, she stays beneath for a long time before re-emerging. She's enjoying herself, laughing and urging me over.

I want to join her and be as cool and carefree as my big sister. But I can't drive Mom's warnings out of my head.

"Don't you ever go swimming at night, you understand me? Ever," she'd told us. And I always listened to Mom. I liked being her good girl, never getting in trouble. Mary hates that about me. But when it comes to being the good daughter or being the fun sister, Mom wins over Mary.

And as much as I know she'll get mad at me for this, I still back away from the water and tell her, "We should go inside before Mom and Dad wake up and find us gone. You know it's not allowed."

"Oh, geez, you're so boring!" she scolds me. I can't see her eyes, but I know she's seething, giving me her death glares.

"Mary, please," I implore. "Let's go back to bed."

"Shut up! Just go!" Her voice is laced with anger, all because I refused. I don't know why she switches on me like that whenever I don't want to do something she's doing.

"You're no fun," she goes on, "always worrying about Mommy and Daddy. Gosh, Reign, no wonder my friends joke about you."

I'm angry. I want to yell at her for making me feel like crap so often, but I don't. I clench my fist and whip around. "Fine!" I grunt and start marching up the sand toward the house.

Seconds later, I hear a loud rush of waves and a beckoning cry. "Reign!" Coughs. "Rei—" Her voice sounds garbled. There's something wrong. I turn on the steps. She's not there. I can't see Mary.

Slowly, I step down on the sand, looking out at the murky water. I want to call her name, but I don't. I'm still so mad at her. Plus, she could be messing with me again.

Her head pushes up. Mary's wailing her hands, splashing about. I yelp, realizing she's further from where she was swimming before. The water's carrying her away.

"Reign!" she manages to yell. Her head goes under again. Seconds after, she comes up coughing, fighting to stay above. It's too hard for her to stay afloat. It's as if the ocean is dragging her under.

Mary's struggling to swim back to shore. She can't. But that's impossible. She's a good swimmer, even on her school's swim team.

"Hel—" *Muffled coughs. Frantic splashes.* "Help!" *Coughs and more coughs.* "Re—" *Coughs.* "Help!"

Oh my God! My sister is drowning. Why aren't I doing something? Why am I just standing here, hopeless, sobbing, not doing anything?

Reign! Do something! Just scream!

"Mom!" I fly out of the dream, crying, drenched in sweat, and my head feels like a construction site.

Mom rushes into my room and hurries to my bedside, taking me into her arms. "Oh, honey. It's only a bad dream."

"I'm so sorry..." I whimper, clinging to her robe. "I should've screamed for help. I should've screamed for you."

"Not this again," she mutters, easing me away. She levels her gaze on my face and says in the sweetest way possible for the umpteenth time, "It's not your fault, honey. It was a terrible accident."

"But I didn't scream for help." I glance down at my sweaty sheets and speak under my breath. "I didn't even scream for her."

She pulls my loose strands out of my face. "Reign, you were in shock. It's time to move on, honey. You can't keep—"

"I was mad at her," I interrupt.

Mom widens her eyes, dips her head, and asks, "What do you mean? Mad at her for what?"

I get up and walk over to the window, moving the teal curtains away to fill the room with more sunlight.

Then I swallow the lump in my throat and tell her something I've concealed all this time. "I was mad at Mary that night. Not just for being upset with me for not getting in the water, but for who she was."

"Who she was?" Mom repeats, coming over to me.

I slump my shoulders as I face her fully. "For being so wild and free, always making jokes and doing fun things. Everybody loved her for that, but they didn't love me. I'm boring Reign, too concerned with what you and Dad think to try anything fun. I was... jealous of her."

"Oh, honey." She cups my face with both hands, her aged eyes piercing mine. "You are far from boring. You're a wonderful, smart, and beautiful young woman, and your dad and I love you very much. What your sister did that night wasn't fun. It was dangerous. And if you had gone in with her, we would have lost you both in that riptide. Oh Reign." She cloaks her arms around me, hugging me tightly. "I may not tell you this often, but even though not a day passes that I don't miss Mary, I'm happy that you're still here."

"You are?" I sob on her shoulder. "You don't wish it was Mary here instead of me?"

"Of course not. Don't you ever think that." She hushes me with a kiss on the side of the head, then adds, "It would be wonderful to have both of my girls together, but I have you. And you are enough. Let go of the guilt, honey. It's time to let it go."

Loosening her grip on me, Mom glances over my face and wipes my cheeks. "I love you, Reign. Don't ever question that."

221

I nod and stifle back the rest of my tears. Mom squeezes my arms, smiles at me, then swivels and starts for the door. In an afterthought, she looks sideways and says, "Take the day off and drive Micah to the bus station."

"Thanks, Mom," I mutter as she slips away, closing the door behind her.

It's Friday. Micah's leaving today. A part of me is nervous and fears he won't come back, but I need to trust that he will.

Going back to the window, I stare out at the ocean. The waves are calm, not as fearful as that night. I inhale and exhale deeply, amble to the dresser, and take out my blue one-piece swimsuit with the thin straps and scoop neckline. It's my second time putting it on since the pool party when Nate asked me if I was twelve.

Jerk.

Before that, I had only looked at this swimsuit when Mom brought it home from one of her shopping trips. I didn't need it then because I wouldn't go into the ocean.

Today's different.

After hauling on my swimsuit, I wear a floral print surplice dress over it and slip into my flip-flops. Today's the day I conquer my fear. I'm going for a swim, and I'm doing it with Micah. It'll be something to motivate him to return.

Pulling up at the beach parking lot, I see Micah perched against the stone wall, dressed in black trunks, a white tee, and black sneakers, ready to go running. He pushes off the wall when I climb out of the car.

"Hey, babe," he says smoothly, meeting me halfway for a kiss. It's soft and lingering. Gliding his eyes all over me, he wrinkles his brows and asks, "No running today?"

I shake my head and tell him, "I'm ready."

His lips curl into a teasing grin. "We've already passed that. Haven't we?"

"Stop." I laugh and playfully jerk his arm. "I mean, I'm ready to go swimming."

"Oh." He glances over his shoulder at the ocean. "Are you sure?" he asks, looking back at me.

"Yes."

I lead him down to the sand and take off my dress and slippers.

"Come with me," I say.

He takes a moment to study my face. Then he kicks off his sneakers and pulls his tee over his head.

"All right."

Micah doesn't push me. He holds my hand and stays with my pace as we approach the water. I stop suddenly, and so does he.

"You okay?" he asks, sounding worried.

I look out into the ocean and see Mary, sunlight bedazzling her skin and dancing on top of the water. Her long, wet, dark strands float all around her.

She's motionless, an unreadable expression on her face as she watches me. I close my eyes for a beat. The night she drowned hits me like electricity, as it always does whenever I try to step into the ocean. Only this time, I have a newfound strength. I refuse to live my life like this. Micah's facing his issues, and so will I.

Opening my eyes, I let out a spurt of air, and for the first time, I say, "I'm fine," and actually mean it.

I release his hand and observe the water as if I'm seeing it for the first time. Pushing back the tension in my tummy, I run forward. Without any fear or regrets, I run.

Micah stays close behind, rushing in with me. I can't believe I'm actually calm, with a steady heart, splashing up seawater. I laugh louder than ever, overjoyed to unchain myself from guilt finally. I peer around, searching for Mary. But she's not here. She's not waiting for me anymore.

She's gone.

"You did it, babe," Micah says, coming up to me. He places his arms around my butt and picks me up above the water, hopping around with me.

Laughter surges from my belly. I stretch my hands over my head, feeling free as I glance up at the sky and take it all in. This moment is unparalleled, and I'm happy to have shared it with him. At this moment, I'm free.

The excitement doesn't end when we slither out of the ocean and collapse on the sand, but it reduces long enough for us to drive back to Micah's place. I keep a smile on as I wash sand and salt off my body, reliving the moment over and over in my head. It still makes me feel giggly, overcoming my fears once and for all. I get a tingling in my stomach thinking about it.

Stepping out of the shower, I slip back into my dress once I dry off. Then Micah and I snack on fruits for breakfast before he starts packing some stuff into a duffle back. The feeling of worry sets in again as I stand by the door and watch him prepare to head back home.

"Are you ready for this?" I ask him as he rests the bag on the arm of the couch.

He glances over his shoulder and smiles halfway. "I am," he replies. "I have to be."

Dropping in a few pairs of socks, Micah zips up his duffle bag and strides over to me, towing me into his arms.

"Are you gonna be okay without me for two days?" he teases, kissing me on the forehead.

"I should ask *you* that. You're the one who has hot babes with crushes back home."

He grins. "You're the only one I have my eye on." My heart flutters as he presses his lips to mine, so soft, sweet, and blissful.

When he eases away, my pounding heart relaxes. I know it's time. I should chill and let him do this.

Micah spins away from me and walks over to get his bag. Draping the strap over his shoulder, he snatches up his keys and cell phone.

"Let's go," he says, coming back to me.

I open the door, and we step outside, lock up, and descend the stairs. Once he secures his bike inside, I drive him to the transportation center, where he'll take a bus to the airport, and from there, he'll board a plane to Colorado.

God! Please let him come back. Please don't let this be a summer fling for us.

"What's on your mind?" he asks as we wait on a bench outside for his bus.

I shake my head. "Nothing." But then admit, "I'm gonna miss you this weekend."

He slings his arm around my back, massaging it. "Wow, I didn't realize you liked me this much."

"As if you don't like me just as much," I shoot back.

"Oh yeah," he laughs.

"Yeah."

We stare at each other for a long while, smiling, trying to unravel the other's thoughts. I wonder if Micah feels as strongly as I do. I wonder if he...

The bus pulls up and draws his attention from me. His face tenses as he moves his hand away and picks up his duffle bag off the pavement.

"Well, here it is," he says, looking back at me as others start making their way onto the bus. "I'll call you when I get there, okay?"

He embraces me in a clinging hug and kisses the side of my head.

"Okay," I whisper.

He kisses me one more time on the lips before he turns to leave. I watch his back as he paces over, falling in line behind the people boarding the bus.

Finally, when it's his time to get on, he glances across to me and smiles, waving bye. Managing a smile, I wave back and allow worry to mask my face after he enters the bus.

"Don't let this be it," I mutter to myself again because, honestly, I think I've fallen for him.

I stand there and watch as the bus takes off, looking to spot Micah at one of the windows. But they're so dark it's hard to see him anywhere.

When the bus disappears down the street, I stride back to my car, and like a fool, I cry. My heart is afraid. I'm so scared I'm not enough, and Haxtun will turn out to mean more to Micah than I do.

THIRTY-THREE

Micah

HAXTUN IS JUST as I left it: a small city with a big heart, as emphasized on the welcome sign. Too bad I didn't feel the "heart" when I ended up in my mess.

Getting out of the taxi in front of Grams' house, I feel a rush of emotions. It would be even better if she were inside waiting for me.

I wasn't sure what to do with the house after leaving juvie. It was all I had left of my grandparents. I couldn't bring myself to sell it.

After a deep breath, I drape the bag over my shoulder and cross the gravel entrance toward the front porch. Swallowing the lump in my throat, I force down the burst of emotions and unlock the dark blue door. Pictures of my grandparents and me hanging on the walls halt my steps, and that homey smell is still present. But that's not the only thing that catches my attention.

It appears someone's been here. The hardwood floor looks polished. I'm sure I left the curtains closed; now they're open, and water's dripping from the tap in the kitchen. Not to mention, there are dishes on the rack. I remember leaving them in the cupboard.

I place my bag next to the door and walk around the living room, seeing if anything else is out of place. It all seems intact, only that it's clean. It is too clean for a house I haven't lived in for a year and a few months.

"Hello?" I call out, confused. I walk to the hallway that leads to the bedrooms and push Grams' door open halfway, peeking inside. Her room is the same as when I left. Nothing has changed in there.

Moving to the guestroom across from hers, I open the door and look inside. My brows fly up at the rumpled sheets on the bed and the suitcase by the closet.

What the hell! Someone's living at my house, and I haven't even sold it.

As if on cue, I hear the front door click open. Anger rushes me. All I want is to give the intruder a piece of my mind for their audacity.

I slip out of the guestroom and march back down the hallway, only to freeze in shock when I come face-to-face with an older version of myself.

"Mitch!" he gasps, as surprised as I am.

"Dad... What are you..." I trail, caught between wanting to hug him and punch him for walking out on Grams and me.

"I didn't know you were coming back," he says, carrying a bag of groceries to the kitchen counter. "Neighbors told me you took off a while back."

I tense up, unable to step forward. "Yeah, well, I'm here now. You can go back to wherever you were."

He pivots and stares at me, a look of regret morphing his wrinkled face. I can't avoid looking into his eyes, the same shade of blue as mine. But man, he's aged. Guess it's the hard life that he's lived.

Dad speaks in a calm tone. "I'm sorry you feel that way, but I'm not leaving, son. This is my house—"

"This is Grams' house," I correct harshly. "You abandoned her."

Striding to the couch, Dad gestures for me to sit down. I stay rooted in the spot.

He starts to speak. "Son, about that—"

"Don't call me that," I snap. "You were never a father to me. You left me to Grams while you went out and got drunk every night, then spent your days passed out somewhere."

"I tried, Mitchel," he defends himself. "I went to rehab."

"Yeah, and how many times have you done that only to give up?"

"Oh, Mitch," he grumbles and massages his temple. "I'm sorry I failed you. But I'm clean now. I haven't had a bottle in five months."

I hold up a hand and gesture for him to stop talking. "Look, I'm not even trying to hear this right now. I have something important to take care of, and when I come back, you better be gone."

He throws his head back as if appalled. I don't care. He's had ample chances in the past, and I'm out of forgiveness for where he's concerned.

I start toward the front door. Dad watches me walk by him. "We should talk, Mitch. There's a lot that we need to work on."

"Not interested," I scoff and storm out the door, slamming it shut behind me.

He has some nerve, wanting to take on the father role in my life now. What if I hadn't come back? Would he have looked for me? Does he know about my time in juvie?

I refuse to think about all that right now. I'm going to call Greg so he can let the Harrisons know I'll be stopping by. I'm focusing my energy on facing Lewis. After that, it's goodbye forever Haxtun.

Chicken shit.

That's how I feel at the moment. I spend a good five minutes outside of Lewis Harrison's brick house, pacing by his red oak tree. I try to think of the right words to apologize for what I've done.

Suddenly, the thought crosses my mind that he's probably going to kick my ass and that this whole wanting to meet is about payback. I didn't even ask Greg if Lewis has spoken to Jason in jail.

Then I start to scold myself for deliberating so much and just man up. There's no way I'm going to come all the way here only to recoil and escape back to Newport. I'm through being that kind of guy. I have to face my past.

Blowing out a long breath, I finally take the steps up to his porch. The door opens before I get the chance to knock. I swallow the lump that's lodged in my throat as I look into the gray eyes of the man I'd hurt two years ago.

Lewis isn't that different from the last time I'd seen him. He still has patches of gray hair on both sides of his head, peeking through his dark strands. Only now, there's a scar on the left side of his forehead, and he appears chunkier and more intimidating.

"Um..." I fumble for words.

"I saw you out here," he says.

"I'm sorry. I wasn't sure what to say, so I thought maybe I shouldn't—"

"It's good you changed your mind," he cuts me off. After a pause, he steps aside and opens the door wider. "Come in, Mitchel."

I manage to move my legs and enter his home. It's not so different from Grams' house, with the living room at the entrance, kitchen and dining room off to the side, and a passage leading to the bedrooms.

"Have a seat," he offers, voice calm.

Walking to the espresso leather couch, I take my time sitting down to conceal my jitters.

"Care for anything to drink?" he asks.

"No, thank you, sir," I reply.

Lewis sits in the armchair and clasps his hands, studying me. "Still so polite. That hasn't changed."

Unable to hold it back any longer, I blurt out, "I'm so sorry about that night. I was angry at my dad. I just... snapped."

He lifts his head slowly and blows out a gush of air. "That's just it, Mitchel. I don't understand why *you,* of all people, hit me. Honestly, I expected Jason to do what he did. He was always a troubled kid. I don't get why you were even friends with him."

"Because everyone else gave up on him, and..." I trail as I consider my words. "I know what it's like for him, not feeling like he's good enough. His parents abandoned him. He got kicked off the baseball team. I just wanted to be his friend."

"But, Mitchel, even though you didn't have your parents growing up, you still had Annie. She did a wonderful job of raising you. Your life is so different from Jason's."

"If we're so different, I wouldn't have hit you," I tell him, my tone sharp.

Lewis eyes the rug. He creases his forehead in deep thought. "I went to see Jason two days ago."

I straighten, surprised by this news. "You did?"

He nods. "Yeah, and let me tell you, he's certainly changed. But there's one thing he said that amazed me."

"What's that?"

Meeting my gaze, the corners of his mouth turn up slightly. "He told me not to blame you, said you were a good friend, and what happened was his fault. Not yours."

"He..." Hearing that, I'm almost out of breath. Jason cursed me the day he was sentenced. He called me a pussy and said I should've finished off Lewis.

"He said that?" I confirm.

Lewis nods. "He did. And it's true. That night, I was disappointed because I knew you were better than that, and I felt sad for Annie. But I also knew something must have gone wrong for you because after Jason nearly killed me, I could hear you next to me when he took off. And I knew you were still good."

"Lewis, I'm so sorry—"

"This isn't about that, Mitchel. The reason why I wanted to see you is because I know you must have felt disappointed in yourself all these years, and you feel like you broke your grandmother's heart, but you didn't."

I suppress my emotions and look down at my hands, trying to remain tough. "I'm sure I did."

"No, you didn't, son. Annie came to see me when I was in the hospital. My wife said she was there until she fell ill."

My eyes expand. "What? She... she visited you?"

"Grace said she was there apologizing, telling her that you were a good boy. That you were only sad in your heart and made a terrible mistake."

I shake my head in dismay. "That definitely sounds like something my grams would do."

"She did it because she loves you. I couldn't be mad at you after that, Mitchel."

There's another pause before he gets up and pats my shoulder.

I stand as well.

Lewis shakes my hand and says, "That's why I wanted to see you, Mitchel. To let you know there's no reason to hold on to the guilt anymore."

"Thank you, sir. This helps a great deal. I appreciate you reaching out. You didn't have to."

"It was necessary for us all to heal." He walks me to the door. "Also, I met your father. Seems he wants to make amends. If you're planning on staying in Haxtun for some time, I suggest working things out with him. At least try."

He opens the door. I step out onto the porch and look back at Lewis. "I'm not staying after tomorrow. There's nothing to work on with my dad."

An unsatisfied expression appears on his face. "Well, that's too bad." He peers down for a second before looking up to meet my gaze again, saying, "Thanks for coming by. All the best with whatever decisions you make from here on."

"Thank you, sir."

We shake hands, and I walk away from Lewis Harrison's house feeling content with that part of my life. Meeting him has made me realize that the past needs to stay in the past. I now have a bright future to look forward to, especially if I have a girl like Reign in it.

Arriving back at Grams' house, I take out my cell phone to call Reign. I need to let her know I met with Lewis and that I'm ready to move on. Only as I step inside, Dad is on the couch waiting for me.

"Why are you still here?" I hiss.

He springs to his feet. "I'm not going anywhere, Mitch. We need to talk."

"I already told you there's nothing to talk about. Just leave. It's what you're good at, anyway."

"You know." He drops his hands on his hips. "You have some nerve coming down on me when you've been in juvie."

I let out a sarcastic laugh. "Oh, so you want to play who has messed up the most? Well, maybe you should remember that if I had a good father in my life, I probably wouldn't have ended up there. Do you ever think about that?"

His mouth clamps shut, and his lips twist from side to side. We fume and glare at each other until his arms fall to his sides, and he says in a softer tone, "I'm sorry. I should have been here for you."

I scoff. "You should have done a lot of things. You should have fought your disease a long time ago. If not for Grams, then for me. And you think just because you're sober now, we'll be cool as a cucumber? It doesn't work like that. There's been years and years of hurt. I'm sorry, but I can't forgive you in just one day."

Lewis could. So, does that make me a hypocrite?

As I veer down the hallway to my room, Dad says to my back, "Please don't leave again, Mitch. We need to work on this."

I stop midstride and throw over my shoulder, "I have to go back. Someone's waiting for me. Someone I know will never treat me the way you did."

"It's not only me that needs your forgiveness, Mitch," he adds as I continue to walk away. When I don't stop, he yells, "Your mother wants to see you!"

THIRTY-FOUR

Reign

I CAN'T JOG for five minutes straight without thinking about Micah. He hasn't called to let me know he's arrived in Colorado, much less sent me a text. It's Saturday, and still, there's no word from him. I wonder what's going on.

After another ten minutes, I turn and head back to my house. What a flimsy workout. I didn't even break a sweat. Running without Micah is hard now.

Dad's in the kitchen making breakfast when I walk through the arched doorway.

"Mom's not up yet?" I ask, slumping over the island.

"She's sleeping in today," he says, not looking at me.

I cross to him at the stove. "Is she okay?"

He shrugs. "Your mom is fine. She wants to stay out of Dean's way while he and his designer make decisions about the restaurant. She's trying to think of her next step, you know?"

"Oh, I was thinking maybe I shouldn't go to work there anymore since she sold it."

"Nonsense," he retorts, turning off the stove. Dad scoops out two large pancakes, handing one of the plates to me. "You should go, work until you leave for your trip at least. Dean says he'll close down for a week or two to make changes, so there's no need to stop before then."

I bob my head slowly and turn my attention to the plate. "Looks good," I say, walking over to the table to sit down.

"Cranberry pancakes," he chuckles. "I remember it's your favorite." He didn't get it wrong.

"Thanks, Daddy." I pour orange juice for us before cutting into the delicious-looking pancake.

"So, will Mom open a smaller restaurant?" I ask as he takes a bite of his own.

Dad swallows before answering, "I don't think so. She doesn't have the love for it anymore. You know, I think she was happier working at that youth center in Providence."

"Hm. Maybe she should consider doing that again."

"Maybe," he echoes and drinks some juice. Setting the glass beside his plate, he switches the conversation to me. "How are things with you and Micah? Why'd he have to leave, anyway?"

"Oh, um..." I sip my juice before I answer truthfully. My parents will find out sooner or later. "Dad, Micah's been in juvie."

His eyes widen as he peers up at me. "What?"

"It was an accident. Something that he's completely sorry for. The man involved asked to see him. That's why he went home. To apologize to him in person."

"Well." Dad rests both hands on the table, his hazel eyes piercing mine. "I can't say I'm okay with you dating him after hearing this."

"Dad, please don't be upset," I implore. "It was an accident, a terrible mistake. Micah's making up for it."

Glancing at his plate, he scratches his chin, exhales deeply, then looks up at me. "You're a smart girl. I know you wouldn't keep someone in your life that wasn't good for you. I trust that you're making the right decision regarding Micah. But promise me, if anything goes wrong, you'll back out of it. You'll let me know if there's trouble."

"Dad." I smile at him. "It's okay. I'm safe with him."

He nods, taking my word for it. "If you say so, Reign."

After breakfast, I shower and peek in on Mom before leaving. The room's dark. She's nestled under the covers, sleeping peacefully. Not wanting to wake her, I quietly back away and head to work.

Pulling into the parking lot at *Captain's Choice*, I finally stop worrying and call Micah. I didn't call sooner since I wanted him to focus on why he was there and give him room to breathe.

He answers on the third ring. "Hey, babe."

My heart speeds up. As pathetic as it might seem, I've missed him in the short time he's been away from me.

"Hey," I manage to say. "You didn't call."

Micah sucks in a long breath before speaking again. "I'm sorry. It completely slipped me."

"Oh." That hurts. Is he forgetting me already? "Okay. How did it go with Lewis?"

"It went fine, better than expected. But something else has happened."

I perk up, curious. "What happened?"

"Well, for one, my dad's been living at my grandmother's house. He claims he's sober now."

"Wow," I mutter, happy to hear that. I know deep down that even though Micah's been hurt by his father constantly dropping in and out of his life, he really does want him there. "That's good."

"Yeah, it's not the only thing, though." His voice comes out low and troubled.

"What else?" I ask, hoping he's all right.

"My mom wants to see me."

"Oh. My. God! Micah..."

"Yeah, that was my reaction, too," he chuckles flatly. "Guess she reached out to my dad."

"Why now? After all these years, she finally wants to meet you?"

Micah pauses for a beat before he answers, "I don't know, Reign."

"Will you meet her?" A part of me selfishly hopes he won't. With both parents suddenly back in his life, Micah might decide to hell with Newport and break up with me.

My heart's pounding more than ever. I'm so scared.

"I don't know that either," he says. "I haven't made up my mind. What do you think?"

What do I think? I grip the phone so hard I'm surprised it doesn't break. I can't tell him the truth. I want him to yell at them for abandoning him and come back to me.

"I... think that decision should be yours," I say. "You should take all the time you need to think about it."

Just make sure when you do make up your mind, you come back to Newport. I need you. I love you.

He sighs into the phone. My breath catches, waiting to hear his next words.

"I feel like I shouldn't leave yet. I should meet her and find out why, you know?"

His reply crushes any hope I have of seeing him on Sunday. I drop my head back on the headrest and close my eyes, forcing the tears away. Guess I won't be picking him up at the transport center tomorrow.

"Okay. My voice sounds strained. I hope he doesn't hear it. "When will you be back then?"

"Probably in a few days," he says. "I want to settle everything here and move on without regrets."

I'm still stuck on *probably*. "Okay." I glance around the lot and then check my reflection in the rearview. My gosh. What if he doesn't want to come back? It'll completely shatter my heart.

"Well, let me know then. I just pulled up at work, so I'll talk to you later. Call me, okay?"

"Okay," he says. I suspect he wants to say more but doesn't.

I want to say more, too, but I don't. I can't say anything, especially since I'm not sure if he's even coming back.

We hang up like that, not saying anything else. An empty feeling forms inside my chest, like I just lost something I can't label. Pushing back more tears threatening to fall, I compose myself and walk into the restaurant.

Dean is here with his overly eclectic designer. She's suggesting painting the light blue interior with more earthy colors like brown or orange. And they want to update the rustic cedar bar to something more modern and funkier. My dad built that bar. Ugh!

The nerve of them.

I leave them to discuss how to replace the aquatic mural on the wall behind the bar and walk out to the deck, where Aislin is cleaning tables and putting up the umbrellas.

Geez. I'm glad Mom decided to stay away while this is taking place because having some stranger come in and change everything you worked hard on must hurt. Then again, she sold *Captain's Choice*. There isn't anything she can do or say.

"What's your mom gonna do after summer?" Aislin asks as I pick up one of her towels to wipe off the chairs.

"She's still making up her mind," I tell her. "What about you? Will you stay and work for Dean?"

She stops what she's doing and walks over to the railing. "John is, but not me. Dean rubs me the wrong way. I can't work for him."

I mosey over and rest my hands on the railing, peering out at sea. "Yeah, I heard him mention something about hiring new workers, anyway."

"Huh," she scoffs. "What a douche."

We stand quietly for a minute before she asks, "Is Micah gone for good? I thought he was going to work until August. Is something wrong with him?"

Her question stirs up the worry again. My eyes pool with tears for the third time. I glance down at my hands to keep her from noticing how scared I am.

Micah might not come back to Newport.

"Um, he had something to take care of in his hometown," I tell her. "He'll be back soon."

When I manage to suppress the tears, I look up at her. Aislin twists her mouth and nods, studying my face.

A moment later, her dark red lips coil into a smile, and her brown eyes light up. "Your birthday's almost here. I heard Clark going over ideas for your cake with your mom. I think you'll love it."

I fake a smile. "I'm sure I will. They did a great job last year."

"Yeah." She smiles back. "Listen, I've been meaning to tell you something. I didn't before because you were still with Nate and wanted to mind my business, but now that you guys have broken up..."

"Just say it," I urge her, more than curious now.

"Well..." She eyes the wooden railing a moment before peering up at me. "The reason why I don't like Nate is because he and my roommate hooked up. She went to a party a few days after you guys graduated, and he happened to be there. She said he kept flirting with her, and she'd had too much to drink. One thing led to another, and they ended up sleeping together."

"You should have told me sooner," I say in a cool tone that implies I'm not upset with her.

"Sorry. You seemed like you wanted things to work with Nate. I thought I'd keep out of it."

"It's fine. It doesn't matter anymore. I would've broken up with him, anyway."

A smile peeks at the corner of her mouth before she asks, "Can I tell you something else?"

Dropping my hands to my hips, I giggle at her. "You're all for confessing today, huh? Go ahead."

Aislin glances across at the bar and eyes John. Looking back at me, she combs her fingers through her pixie cut and says in a girlish way, "I'm scared I'll lose him to Claudia."

I narrow my eyes, look at John, and carry my gaze back to Aislin. "Oh my gosh. How did I not see it?"

The soft glances. The way she'd defend him to Mom whenever he was late. The way she'd smile for no reason when she walked by him at the bar. The way she watched him with Claudia at the barbecue like a jealous girlfriend.

Aislin likes John. A lot.

"You have to tell him!" I blurt out excitedly.

She fidgets and bites her bottom lip, rocking back and forth on her heels. "I can't. I'm scared. What if he doesn't like me in that way? What if I ruin our friendship by confessing? And your best friend is hot. I'm sure he'll go for her—"

"Okay, first, Claudia's not interested in John. She's already preoccupied with trying to win back a previous boyfriend. Secondly, how will you know he doesn't feel the same if you don't make a move?"

She chews at the inside of her mouth and gazes at him again. As if he senses her watching, John peers up from the drinks menu and catches her looking. Aislin quickly drives her eyes back to me.

I want to laugh. She's so cute, so vulnerable, so not the tough girl she often portrays.

"I can't," she says. "I'm not that brave."

"Neither am I."

She lifts a brow as if I'm full of shit. "Yeah, right. You dropped Nate for Micah."

Something plunges in my stomach. I want Micah here with me so bad. I want him to hurry and make up his mind, take care of his past, and return to me.

"Yeah, well," I mutter. "Didn't want to stay unhappy with Nate. I made a choice. I still don't think it was the wrong one, either."

"Good for you," she replies with a grin. "I hope I'll find my courage, too."

"You will."

I glimpse Dean out of the corner of my eye. He walks out onto the deck. "Ladies, how about we save the girl talk for later and actually get some work done?"

Aislin looks at him with a scowl. The tough side I'm familiar with resurfaces as she parts her lips to say something. "Listen, you—"

"Sorry," I cut her off. "We'll get back to work." I know her remark would have been snarky, so I'm probably saving her from getting fired.

She flashes him a fake smile before turning to go back to wiping off tables. I do the same.

Claudia comes over to my house in the late hours. We lie in my bed as she rambles on about our trip to Miami, where we'll be staying, and when we can go shopping for bathing suits.

"Now that you're over your fear, I think it's time we get you some skimpies." Her word for sexy bikinis.

"I don't feel like wearing a bikini. I don't want to send the wrong message to guys down in Miami," I tell her.

She knocks my arm lightly. "It's not even about that. It's about celebrating your liberation. You have a great body. Flaunt it, even if you're not single."

"Hmm," I mumble.

"What does that mean?"

I pick up the extra pillow and huddle it on my stomach. "I spoke to Micah today. I think you were right about him not coming back."

She pushes up on her elbow and rests her head in the palm of her hand. "I told you to forget about what I said—"

"He already met with Lewis. The thing is, his father's back, and he might reunite with his mother, too."

"Oh, that's wonderful," she perks up. "And what did you say after hearing this?"

"I told him to take some time to think about it."

"He should. So, what's he going to do?"

I turn my head and look at her. "He doesn't think he should leave yet. Guess he's going to meet her."

Claudia lies on her side. "I see why that worries you."

"Yeah. I feel so selfish. I'm hoping he'll stay mad at them and leave, but at the same time..."

"You want him to be happy because you've noticed something's missing in his life."

I nod. "There's definitely a missing piece in his heart."

After a brief pause, she squeezes my hand. "Let him do this and come back to you. I'm sure he'll even make it back in time for your birthday."

I sigh. "Hope so. If he doesn't, then I don't think he's coming back. Ever."

THIRTY-FIVE

Micah

I'VE KEPT my distance from Dad for the past few hours so I can think long and hard about what he said about my mother. I should leave today, but part of me wants answers to questions I've secretly asked all these years.

At the crack of dawn, he comes banging on my door. "Mitchel, we need to talk, son. I won't let you take off today without settling things."

What the hell! He *won't* let me take off?

Throwing the sheets aside, I spring out of bed, haul on a t-shirt over my sweatpants, and yank the door open. "Where is she? Where has she been? Why now?"

He backs up a tad with his hands raised. "She's going to answer all your questions when you see her."

"So she's been in Haxtun all this time and hasn't tried to see me once?"

"Mitch, please." He waves around the room. "You've been cooped up here since yesterday. At least eat something, and then we can talk about her."

I pause for a fraction of a second and start out of my room. "Fine."

Dad follows me down the passage. I plop down at the small dining table as he goes to the stove.

"I remember you didn't care much for eggs, so I made bacon and toast alone. Is that okay?" he asks over his shoulder, lifting a frying pan off the stove.

I nod and say dryly, "Yeah, that's fine." At least he remembers something about me.

He scoops bacon onto a plate with toast and brings it over to the table, setting it down before me.

After fixing a plate for himself, he sits down across from me. "There's coffee in the pot or milk in the fridge. Help yourself."

I'm so curious about her that I can't even eat. I've always wondered what she's like. Why didn't she want me?

Dad takes a bite out of his buttered toast and peers up at me. "Eat something," he urges.

"Did you know where she was all this time?" I ask. "Did Grams?"

He places the rest of his toast back on the plate and swallows before answering. "I didn't. I can't speak for your grams, though. She kept things from me."

"Oh gee, I wonder why," I snort, picking up bacon.

Dad wrinkles his forehead and glances at the kitchen counter, falling into deep thought. A few seconds later, he mutters, "I really let her down, huh?"

Turning back to me, he resumes eating his breakfast, saying before he shoves the rest of his toast inside his mouth, "You should bring flowers to her grave since you're here."

His words hit a nerve. I stop eating, get up, and walk over to the coffee pot. I should do that. I felt so bad about not being at home when she was sick that I didn't dare to visit her grave after my release.

Dad's right. I need to bring her flowers and free *that* guilt off my chest.

"Are you still leaving today?" he asks me when I return to the table after filling a mug.

"I don't know," I tell him, sitting down.

"So, you'll meet your mother then? I mean, you say you want answers, and only she can give them to you."

I drink a little before I put the mug down next to my plate. "Where does she live?"

He dips his head, appearing regretful. "She... um... only five minutes from here."

"What?" I scoff in my amazement. "Has she always been that close? Did you know?"

His thick brows shoot up. "Mitch, of course not. I wouldn't keep that from you."

"Right, 'cause if you knew, you would've just left me back at her doorstep and gotten one little trouble off your hands, huh?"

Dad scrunches up his face and falls back on the chair, exhausted. "That's not true."

"Seemed that way when I was a kid," I retort, sipping more coffee.

"I was happy to have a son, and I wanted to be a good father to—"

"But you just couldn't," I cut him off. "You had to choose between me and the bottle. I wasn't worth it." My chest hurts. Anger fills me as I continue speaking. "Do you have any idea what it's like being neglected by both of your parents? My mother abandoned me to my alcoholic father, and he abandoned me for alcohol. I felt like shit, and I kept that in all these years."

"I'm so sorry, son." His eyes turn glossy. He releases a razor-sharp breath and leans forward, resting his elbows on both sides of his plate. "I had a disease, Mitchel. I needed help. Since I've gotten it, I've become a better person. All I'm asking for is a chance to prove it."

"Just give me her address so I can go see her. Then I'll be out of your hair and hers." I finish the rest of my toast and bring the plate to the sink.

After I wash up the breakfast dishes and start to head down the passage toward the bathroom, Dad calls out, "I hope you'll consider staying. This is your home, Mitch. You belong here."

"Maybe if Grams was still here," I reply with my back turned.

Dad pulls his car up at a light blue, raised ranch with shrubs along the edge of the clean-cut lawn.

"This is it," he tells me. His voice makes me shudder, unleashing a bunch of nerves in my stomach. I can't believe I'm actually going to meet my mother. After so many years, I'm going to see the face of the woman who didn't want me.

What do I say to her?

Do I even want to give her the chance to get to know me now?

What's the point?

She's lost out on almost twenty years.

Without looking at Dad, I open the door and step out of the car, taking a breath before walking up to the gate.

"I'll be here, waiting," he says as if he's assuring me of his support. I never had it before, and I certainly don't need it now.

Glancing back, I huff a laugh and give him the 'really' stare before continuing to the entrance.

When I approach the red-painted front door, I lift my hand, lingering for a beat before I finally knock. I step back, stick my hands in my jeans pockets, and wait.

Shortly after, the door clicks open, and a girl looks at me. She's almost my height, probably around fifteen or sixteen, with long blonde hair. She stares at me with curiosity in her blue eyes. They're the same shade as mine, like my mother's.

I have a sister.

"Can I help you?" she asks, tilting her head to the side.

"I... um," I stop to clear my throat and say the name I haven't spoken since I was ten, since the day Dad told me in one of his drunken episodes that she didn't want me, "I'm looking for Karen."

She twists and calls over her shoulder, "Mom! Someone's here to see you."

"Who is it?" I hear the woman answer.

Footsteps approach. My whole body tenses. As she comes around the corner, my heart starts to race. For a moment, I consider bolting for the car and pretend that I never came here. But then she strides up to the door and looks me dead in the eye. I freeze in place.

"My God..." She covers her mouth with both hands and stares at me bug-eyed.

There she stands. My mother.

"Mom, are you okay?" asks her daughter. My sister. "Who's this?" She glances at me and then at my mother.

"Please, come inside," Mom says, opening the door wider. My sister steps aside so I can enter, confusion imprinted on her porcelain face.

I enter and peer around. My mother's been living well. She has a lovely home and a family.

So why didn't she want me?

"Would you like some coffee?" she offers.

I shake my head and say flatly, "No thanks."

My sister is still looking back and forth from our mother to me, trying to decipher what's going on. She folds her arms at her waist and eyes me intently.

Touching her daughter's arm, Mom says calmly, "Why don't we all sit down first?" She looks at me, adding, "Then we can talk."

Obediently, I follow them into the living room and sit on the couch, squeezing my knuckles. I'm boiling over with questions, yet I decide to be considerate of my sister, who clearly doesn't know she has a brother.

Mom sits in the armchair, and her daughter settles on an ottoman beside her. My sister creases her forehead and brushes back her long hair behind her ears, crossing one leg over the other.

"Okay, what's going on?" she asks, her soft voice laced with concern.

"Cassie, this is Mitchel," Mom introduces. "He's my son. Your brother."

My sister raises her thin brows and angles her head. "What? Brother? Mom, how can that be?"

Glancing at Cassie, Mom explains, "I had Mitchel before meeting your father." She looks at me as she continues. "I wasn't in a position where I could take care of you. That's why I gave you to your father and grandmother."

"But why didn't you ever come to see me? Why did you wait all these years to reach out?" I ask sharply.

She shakes her head, remorseful. "You looked so happy with your grandmother. I'd watched you on several occasions: on the playground and when you'd be in town with her. She loved you and took much better care of you than I could. I didn't want to interrupt your lives and take you away from her."

I rake my hand through my hair, displeased with her answer. "So you pretended I was never born, married someone, not to mention had a daughter, yet you couldn't bring yourself to see me once? To let me know who you were. You didn't have to take me. I was fine with my grandmother. But at least to see me. To let me know you exist. See what you look like. Or to tell me that you didn't leave because you didn't want me."

"I'm so sorry, Mitchel. The truth is, I was afraid. I felt like I didn't deserve to see you," she says, tears stinging her eyes. She reaches out and brushes Cassie's cheek, telling her, "I'm sorry I didn't do this sooner."

Cassie pulls away from her touch, glances at me, then stands. "I can't do this... I have volleyball practice."

She turns and hurries from the living room. Mom calls out to her. "Cassie, please stay! We should talk about this."

Regardless of Mom's pleas, my sister's already out the door. She slams it shut, and I can hear her footsteps bustling down the front steps.

Straightening in the armchair, Mom eyes my face in awe, studying my features. "You hardly look like me. You have my eyes, but everything else is your father."

I lower them from her so I can find the strength to ask, "Why are you reaching out now? Why, after so many years?"

She leans forward and reaches a hand out to touch mine. "Because I finally found the courage to see you. I know I'm terribly late, but I still want you to know that it was hard leaving you with your father. I only did it because I loved you and wanted the best for you." She sniffles. "I love you, Mitchel. Seeing you now, I don't feel guilty anymore because Annie raised you right. You turned out pretty good."

The guy I became, the guy I am, can't hate her. I don't even know what I want from her. It certainly isn't for her to fall into the role of being my mother. I'd already received that from Grams.

Maybe I came here for the reason and the answer she just gave me. Suddenly, I feel like that's enough.

Content, I rise to my feet to take off. Mom gets up as well. I start to leave when she touches my arm and says, "Will you come by for dinner tomorrow? My husband will be back from his business trip, and he'd love to meet you. I told him about you."

Glancing at her, I start to refuse when she cuts me off. "I'd love for you and your sister to talk." She's asking for a lot. What should I do?

"I don't know," I tell her. "I have to go back to Rhode Island."

She blinks, surprised. "That's where you were? Are you going to school there?" A smile crosses her lips despite how flabbergasted she is now. "Gosh, I should have asked you all those things, like what you're into, favorite food, if you're dating anyone—"

"I am," I sputter. "She's waiting for me there."

"Oh, I see..."

I gesture to the front door. Mom stops me again. "At least stay a few more days. Please, Mitchel. I know I have no right to ask anything of you. This is all I'm asking—that you stay for a few more days. For Cassie... for me?"

Reign will be upset. I promised her I'd return soon. But I've just met my mother and a sister I never knew I had. Dad's back in my life. Maybe I should stay a while longer, at least until I feel satisfied enough to leave.

With a deep breath, I press my eyes shut for a beat, open them, and tell her, "Okay, only a few more days."

Smiling at me, Mom hesitantly reaches in for a hug. She decides against it when she realizes I'm not reciprocating. I turn to walk out the door but change my mind.

I'm tired of being mad at people when someone like Lewis Harrison could forgive after what happened to him.

If my parents are trying to make amends, then it's time for me to let go of the hurt, too. That's the only way I can leave Haxtun burden-free.

I turn back to her and give her a gentle hug. Her embrace is warm and loving. The scent of her perfume, light and floral, is soothing.

We hold on to each other like lifelines for what seems like forever. When we pull away, I realize her eyes are glistening. There's moisture around mine, and I smile.

Something breaks apart inside my heart. All the hurt, mistrust, hatred, and misunderstanding fall away. Peace settles instead.

Opening the door, I glance back at her. Her manicured hand bends in a half-wave. I repeat her gesture. It's not just her hug I've craved. It's her.

My mother.

I have to stay and learn more about her and my sister, as well as spend time with my dad. They might not be perfect, but they are my family. I need to do this. Before I leave Haxtun, I have to leave whole.

I hope in my heart that Reign will understand.

THIRTY-SIX

Reign

"DON'T CRY," I whisper to myself for the hundredth time while standing in front of the dresser mirror in my room. I'm wearing my blue, sleeveless fit-and-flare cutout dress that falls a little above my knees. My loosely curled hair let down in my back, and I'm wearing heels for the first time in months.

It's my birthday. My family and friends are downstairs waiting for me, but I'm not feeling happy.

Micah is still not back from Colorado, and I don't understand why. He said he wouldn't stay because I'm not there. So why is it hard for him to leave?

Perhaps he's mending his relationship with his father and building one with his mother. Whatever the case, I haven't heard from him in a week. He doesn't seem to care that he's missing my birthday.

"Ugh." I blow out a sharp breath and straighten my posture. I don't want to ruin tonight wallowing in sadness. I want to smile and be grateful to everyone for helping me celebrate.

Stepping out of my room, I meander downstairs with a smile on my face. Everyone's in the living room: my parents, Mrs. Norman, Aislin, John, Chef Clark, Claudia, her dad Andre and stepmom Eleanor. They're all waiting for me with broad smiles plastered on their faces.

I stand in the arch doorway, taking in the moment and mentally telling myself that I won't feel sad. Micah isn't here, but I won't feel sad.

"Oh honey, look at you," Mom gushes. She strides over to hug me. "You're beautiful, birthday girl," she says, kissing my forehead.

"Gosh, you're growing up," Dad says, walking over. "You mind if I still call you my little girl, even though you're nineteen now?"

Dad cloaks me in his big bear hug, which always comforts me. I need it right now.

"I'll always be your little girl," I tell him.

"Happy birthday," he cheers, and everyone else follows.

"Okay, okay." Claudia hauls me over to the couch. She plops down beside me, handing me a gift. "Open mine first," she pleads, her eyes sparkling like a disco ball.

I take the box from her and glance at her face, a bit hesitant to see what it is. "It's nothing inappropriate, right?" I chuckle.

Laughter breaks out in the room. She lightly jerks my arm. "No, silly. Actually, I would have, but your parents are here, too."

Her dad clears his throat, and Eleanor scoffs, flipping her hair off her shoulder. "Gosh."

I cut my eyes from her to open Claudia's gift. It's a sweet feminine collection, which includes a body lotion, shower gel, body mist, bronze charm bangles, and matching earrings.

"Aw, Claudes." I lean in and kiss her cheek. "This is so sweet. Thank you."

"You're very welcome."

While everyone's showering me with gifts, I notice that Dad slips out of the living room. He returns shortly with something large and rectangular, concealed in yellow wrapping paper.

"Whoa, Dad. What's this?"

He and Mom are grinning at each other sneakily.

"Hope you like it," Dad says as he sets the gift down at my feet on the rug.

Mom rests her hand on his shoulder. They both smile at me as I begin to peel off the wrapping paper.

My mouth drops when I see what it is. "Dad! So this is why you told me to stay out of the workshop."

He shrugs, acting modest.

I beam at the antique-looking oak wood treasure chest. I notice he's added his unique touch to it. My name's carved into the lock, and there are sunflower designs on the inside and out, which happens to be my favorite flower.

My heart flutters when I notice the picture of me and Mary at the bottom of the chest. She was seven, and I was five at the time. Written at the bottom of the picture in her handwriting is a funny line Mary used to say to me:

You can always Reign on my parade, little sissy.

I stifle back tears of joy, straightening to hug Dad. "Thank you, Daddy," I breathe into his chest. Then I tow Mom in, and the three of us clutch each other.

It's nice not feeling guilty while thinking about Mary. And I'm more than happy that my parents decided to put out her photos again without worrying they'd upset me. We can all have some closure.

Once we pull apart, Mrs. Norman switches on indie music, and everyone shuffles about, indulging in Chef Clark's exquisite food and drinks.

As the night progresses, I stop thinking about Micah long enough to push myself to entertain and appreciate my guests. Oddly, I end up talking to Eleanor, Claudia's stepmom. It is rare for me since I find her so uptight, and she always manages to make everything about her.

I hate how when she talks to people, she eyes you from head to toe as if she's horrified at how cheap your attire compares to hers. And Eleanor never wears anything that's less than a hundred dollars, so it's no wonder she's frowning at my thirty-dollar dress from Marshalls.

"If Claudia had reminded me sooner, I would have picked up a nicer gift for you in Italy," she says with a pretentious smile, showing off her pearly whites. I'll never complain about the designer handbag she gave me. "Gosh, it's such a beautiful country," she goes on. "I just didn't want to leave."

Then why did you? I wanted to ask her. Instead, I smile and nod politely. I spot Aislin over her shoulder and notice she's looking frazzled because John isn't paying her much attention.

I direct Eleanor to her. "Have you met Aislin? She's interested in visiting Italy; she studies all things Italy in school. I'm sure she'll love to hear about your trip."

Eleanor perks up. "Is that so?" She twists and starts toward Aislin without even excusing herself from me. Whatever.

Quietly sneaking out of the living room, I walk around to the passage and sit on the built-in seat under the staircase. I don't think I can keep up the façade much longer. My heart's too sad.

Within seconds, Mom steps out of the kitchen, glimpsing me on her way to the living room.

"Why are you hiding out here by yourself?" she asks, coming over with a glass of wine in one hand and a plate of crab cakes in the other.

I shake my head but say nothing.

She sits beside me, offering me a crab cake. "They're really good. Clark made them."

"I'm not that hungry," I reply in a low tone. "Thanks, though."

She sets her glass and the plate down on the small table beside the seat and then shifts back to me.

"Oh honey, what's the matter? It's a nice dinner. Not too big, not too small."

"No, it's great. Thank you." Resting my head against the wood, I sigh deeply before telling her the truth. "Micah's not here. He's not coming back."

She's quiet for a moment. Then she says, "I'm sorry, Reign. But I'm sure he has his reasons, and you'll probably see him once he sorts out everything. Don't get too upset over it."

"I don't think so," I breathe out. "He saw his dad again after so long, and he's meeting his mom for the first time. He'll probably want to stay there and get to know them."

Pursing her lips, Mom reaches over to stroke my hair. "I hate that you're so sad on your birthday. I wish I could do something."

"No, I'm sorry for being this way. I should suck it up and enjoy myself. You and Dad put this together for me. I'm being selfish."

"You don't have to force yourself," she retorts, touching my shoulder. "But at least come and cut your cake. I swear Clark outdid the last one. It'll definitely cheer you up, if only for tonight."

She stands first, sticking her hand out for me to take it. "Come on, honey."

I push from the seat. She takes up her drink and the plate, and we head for the living room, pausing as someone rings the doorbell.

My heart smashes against my ribcage. Excitement soars within me. I glance at Mom and look at the door, swallowing hard. She pulls away from me to answer it. I remain by the arched doorway, anticipation building up fast.

I don't see who it is when Mom opens the door, and I don't peer around her. I wait. As she throws her head back in surprise, I figure it isn't Micah after all. She steps aside, and Nate passes her, obliterating what little hope I had left.

"Happy birthday," he says, handing me a small gift. He inches closer when I don't take it. His eyes glide over my body, and he swallows. "You look lovely."

"I'll leave you two alone," says Mom, closing the front door and walking into the living room.

I look up at him, confused. "What are you doing here? Did my mom invite you?"

He shakes his head. "No. I remembered your birthday. I had to get you something."

My stomach tenses. "But why?"

"You know why, Reign." He fills the distance between us and places a hand at my elbow.

I step away from him. "You have to go. Micah—"

"Isn't even here," he cuts me off. "By the way, I looked up that loser. He's been in juvie for school vandalism and for hitting someone. He's obviously violent."

"He's not," I hiss. "I know who he is, and he's nothing like that."

His jaw stiffens. His eyes become cloudy. "You know about that? You *know,* and you still want to be with him and not *me*? I gave you time to think it over, to think about what you're doing, and you still haven't come to your senses."

Even though he's clearly upset with me, he keeps his voice low.

"I'm sorry," I tell him. "I can't help the way I feel."

Nate drops his hands to his side, still clutching the gift. His lips quiver as he searches for his next words.

He catches his breath before managing to speak again. "You've really hurt me, you know that?"

I stay quiet, unsure of how to respond.

He sputters a sarcastic laugh. "I didn't even realize I loved you this much until I lost you." He lowers his eyes to the hardwood for a moment, looks at me one more time, and starts for the door.

"I'm sorry, Nate," I mutter at his back. "I'm really sorry."

Opening the door, he lingers there and places his gift on the table next to it. "I know. You can't help the way you feel." He steps outside and closes the door behind him, leaving me with guilt and, at the same time, relief. Because I think now more than ever, he'll find a way to move on from me.

THIRTY-SEVEN

Micah

WHEN I RIDE up to the house, I see Nate hop in his car and drive off. He seems upset. Why was he at Reign's birthday party? I ease off my bike, take her gift out of my pants pocket, and walk up to the entrance. As I approach the door, I glimpse her in the window of the living room.

She's laughing, cutting her beachy-looking birthday cake—which has flip-flops and a dolphin on top of it—as everyone cheers for her. Reign's parents hug her with pride. She's beautiful. Happy without me.

The thought occurs—maybe someone like me shouldn't be with a girl like Reign, a girl so innocent and untainted.

Suddenly, I'm afraid to face her, fearful I might ruin her night. She's probably upset with me for not coming back when I said I would, and now I show up and want to pick up where we left off.

How presumptuous of me.

Maybe she doesn't want to be with such a complicated guy. Perhaps I don't deserve her. I'm just not good enough for Reign.

Doubt clouds my mind so much I start to back away from the house, walking down the concrete toward my bike. I glance at her small gift in my hand, a necklace with our initials, and stick it back in my pocket, towing my bike away from her house.

"Micah?"

Chills run down my back. I freeze in my tracks and peer back nervously. My God, she's stunning. In fact, it's frightening how gorgeous this girl is.

Reign walks toward me. I park my bike and meet her halfway. She glances over my appearance as if to make sure I'm really here, then draws in a deep breath. "You jerk. I didn't even know you were coming back, yet you were leaving again without saying a word. I don't understand. Why were you leaving? Why didn't you come inside?"

"I thought you didn't want to see me," I tell her, feeling like a complete ass. "I thought that... you were happy without me."

"*Happy*?" she repeats, sounding insulted. "I've been anything but happy for the last couple of days without you, Micah."

"I'm sorry. That's my fault. I'm truly sorry—"

"I love you!" she blurts out, her body shivering as she pierces my soul with her beautiful eyes. "I've been wondering for a while what exactly this is, but I'm sure of it now. I love you, and I..." She stops talking as tears trickle down her cheeks. "I hope you can love me too—"

I crush her mouth with a hungry kiss. I couldn't hold back any longer, especially after hearing her say she loved me.

Holding on to her for dear life, I kiss her some more, satisfying the wait we've both had to endure. Man, I've missed the sugary taste of her mouth and the addictive scent of her body.

Her ferocious grip on me sends lightning bolts through my veins. All I want is to kiss her and make love to her until I have nothing left because I feel the same way. And I need to overcome the feeling that I don't deserve something so good.

Easing her out of my arms, I catch my breath and say at last, "I love you, too."

She smiles from ear to ear and shakes her head slowly. "You do?"

"Of course I do, silly."

I kiss her again. This time, we move without haste, only to break apart when her Dad calls out.

"Reign, you all right, honey?"

Mrs. Aldridge steps down the entrance. She slows in her steps once she sees me. "Well, I'll be..." She smiles. "I'm glad you're back, Micah."

"Hey, Mrs. Aldridge." I wave awkwardly. From Reign's smeared lips, I'm sure her lipstick is all over my mouth.

Mrs. Aldridge starts to head back inside. "Well, you two come in then. We're about to play some games."

I look at the door. Mr. Aldridge nods at me before slipping back inside the house.

"Is your dad mad at me?" I ask Reign, refocusing on her.

"No." Smiling, she wipes lipstick off my mouth with the palm of her hand. "Are you scared of facing him?"

"I kind of am," I admit.

She takes my hand and tows me toward the house. "It'll be fine."

"Oh, wait," I stop her, taking her gift out of my pocket. "This is for you. Happy birthday, baby."

A melting smile appears as she opens the box and takes out the silver necklace with our initials. "Aw, Micah. This is beautiful. Thank you." She kisses me.

I shake my head as I put it on for her. "No, thank you."

Turning her to face me again, I lower for another sweet kiss. Then we start walking.

As we approach the concrete entrance and make our way to the front door, she asks me, "How was it meeting your mom for the first time?"

I slide my arm around her waist as we step inside, answering after a long breath, "It was good. I'll tell you all about it later."

Reign kisses me on the cheek before we enter the living room and join the others.

Everyone welcomes me happily. I even spot Reign's parents, their arms around each other, smiling as they look over at us.

I left Haxtun after reconnecting with my parents and making friends with my sister. I received forgiveness from Lewis and said goodbye to my grams. All the way to Rhode Island, all I could think about was this incredible girl, this young woman. Reign. And the way she makes me feel.

How I'm complete, I'm me, the man I am and want to be, when I'm with her.

Now more than ever, I feel at ease and accepted into her circle of family and friends. I feel as if I'm right where I belong.

Reign

THERE AREN'T too many changes when Claudia and I return from Florida two weeks later. *Captain's Choice* still has its name. Aislin decided to stay on board since John and Clark, including Micah, are going to keep working there. Dean's letting him stay after summer onward.

They've changed the interior to orange and made the outside dark but left the cedar bar and mural alone. Dean's worked with Clark to add a few more options to the menu, and they've added a little platform for live acoustic performances. I think that's the best move because artists like Allysen Callery can perform. The place has certainly become busier since that addition.

Mom finally decided to go back to working as an advisor for teens. She'll be joining the youth center in Newport this fall. She seems more relaxed these days without the stress of owning a restaurant. And she's taken up a new hobby with Dad: Yoga. Mom enjoys it. Dad's still getting the hang of stretching his body so much.

As for me, I can't believe I'm a few days away from starting my first year in college. I'm bubbling over with anticipation. It's a new chapter of my life that I'm happy to take on, and even more thrilled that Micah is there with me.

I love that he's been talking about his dreams more openly, sharing things with me he was cautious about before, like how he's thinking about being a fitness instructor and even considering going to college next year.

He talks about his family a lot more, too, telling me about his sister and how he'll travel to Haxtun now and then to visit her and his parents.

So much has happened between the two of us and in our individual lives over this summer alone.

I never imagined ever getting over my fear of going into the ocean or not feeling guilty over Mary's death. But here I am, spending the radiant Sunday morning sailing around Newport Harbor on Aster with Micah. Claudia and Ryan are with us. They finally talked, and Ryan realized she was the girl he truly wanted to be with. John made that step as well, confessing his feelings to Aislin and finally putting her nerves at ease. They're sailing with us. Who knew life could turn out so great?

The emotions I have are indescribable. No words could sum up just how happy I am, and I feel I owe that a great deal to Micah.

He glances at me with a huge grin on his gorgeous face as if he can read my mind. I don't doubt it because the love we have is magical. In a sense, it's like no other. It sparks a burst of electricity in my tummy. It strengthens me. Empowers me to take on my challenges.

This kind of feeling is undeniable. Incomparable. Real.

It's our kind of love.

ACKNOWLEDGMENTS

To my wonderful family and friends, thank you so much for all your love and support. Tim, thank you for making me believe in love again and for being a shoulder to lean on. Thanks for your suggestions. To you, it's not much, but you have no idea how much I value your input.

Ms. Laurie Treacy, thank you for the lovely comments and encouragement. Your critique is indescribable. You certainly help to bring my stories to life. Thank you. Thank you.

Finally, to you, reader, thank you for taking the time. I will forever appreciate your support of anything I write. Your feedback motivates me to improve my craft and keep writing. I cannot say thank you enough. My only gift to every one of you is providing you with stories worth reading, and hopefully, they are. Do let me know.

ABOUT THE AUTHOR

Shane Morgan is the author of contemporary romance, suspense, and fantasy books. She lives in Rhode Island with her amazing husband, where she spends her days writing and escaping into stories.

www.shanemorganwrites.com
Facebook.com/authorshanemorgan
Instagram.com/shanemwrites
Twitter.com/shanemwrites